Kind
Lies

Ann Eichenmuller

HighTide
Publications, Inc.

High Tide Publications, Inc.
1000 Bland Point Road
Deltaville, Virginia 23043
www.HighTidePublications.com

Edited by: Narielle Living (NarielleLiving@gmail.com)
Cover by: Firebelliedfrog@gmail.com

Publisher's Note: This is a work of fiction. Names, characters, businesses, places, events and incidents are either the products of the author's imagination or used in a fictitious manner. Locales and public names are used for atmospheric purposes. Any resemblance to actual persons, living or dead, or to businesses, companies, institutions, actual events or locales is purely coincidental.

First Edition: March 26, 2017
BISAC: FIC022100 Mystery and Detective - Amateur Sleuth
FIC022040 Mystery and Detective - Women Sleuths
Printed in the United States of America
ISBN: 978-1945990-80-9

To Eric, my love

To Ame & Janet

Ann Eichenmuller

Prologue

THE WATER FLOWS QUICKLY BENEATH the bridge that separates Assateague Island from the mainland. The wind has been onshore for the better part of a week, swelling this normally shallow river so that the tide creeps over the seawall and crawls across the grass of the shore. The fisherman has come early this season, giving into a yearning to smell the salt air.

He is an old man, and he has recently had the sense that age is stalking him. Though he does not say it aloud, it was this ominous feeling that led him, somewhat impulsively, to plan a fishing trip in March. Then, too, he is tired of the perpetual charcoal-colored grime of the city that stains his siding, his windows, and his car. Sometimes he imagines it is staining his lungs as well, invading his mouth and nose with every breath.

He came at slack tide, around two in the afternoon. Because he listened to NOAA this morning, he knew that they were calling for two feet over high water, so he had come prepared, wearing his white rubber watermen's boots and carrying a large thermos of hot coffee. The west shore park was a good spot on a cold day, wind-sheltered from the east by the dunes of the island. The visitor's center was closed, but they left out a portable toilet and a few picnic tables on the bank, and there was a small dock you could set up on to fish. The sun had even come out for a piece, warming his hands and face.

But now it is after five, and the tide is running out. He watches weeds and the occasional scrap of trash swim by him, heading toward the sea, in what little light remains of the day. Low clouds are pushing in from the ocean, and he feels his joints begin to ache from the chill air and the long hours of inactivity.

The road crew that has been working on the bridge all day has gone, knocking off at around four. He was glad at first. He hooked only three fish all day, none large enough to keep, and he thought at first the noise was to blame. They were using a jackhammer to break up the surface of one lane of the two-lane bridge and then hauling up the chunks of concrete with heavy equipment. It was more than enough to scare anything away. Still, they were something to watch when nothing was biting. One of the work trucks had stopped by before they left, and several of the men had come over to see how he had fared, making small talk about lures and hooks and the catches of springs past.

Anyway, he thinks, it wasn't the noise after all. He is doing no better now, not a single tug on the line in the hour since they left. Even the wind has died, leaving a kind of deathly stillness that has been broken only by the sounds of a car and motorcycle as they drove by some fifteen or twenty minutes ago.

He briefly wondered at that, as there was not much else to do.

The workers left one of those automatic lights on the bridge with some kind of motion sensor. When they stopped to chew the fat with the fisherman they laughed about it, because as far as they could see, it would have been easier to close it. The other side was all government-owned park land, and both the campground and the beach access didn't open up until the first of April. The road itself dead-ended at the park gate. But some paper-pusher in an office told them to put up the light, so they that's what they did. It was a half-hour of easy work after a long day, so they weren't complaining.

Why would anyone be going across the bridge now, just before sunset? It must be teenagers, the old man thinks, out partying, drinking beer or doing drugs or whatever else kids do these days. He hopes they won't come back and bother him, and the thought of it frightens him just a little.

He checks his watch again, and then his cell phone. No bars.

Perhaps it is time to go.

The fisherman is not afraid of being alone; he has been alone for most of the past eighteen years. Still, it is different to be by yourself outdoors after dark, when even places you know well become clothed in unfamiliar shadows. At his age, he knows he is a target for lots of things, not the least of which are unpredictable adolescents. He reels in his line, puts away his lure, and closes up his tackle box. Just as he is folding his chair, he hears the sound of an engine. By the time he looks up, all he can see are tail lights. He thinks he recognizes it as the motorcycle. It is obviously headed back toward town, and he feels a mild relief.

It takes him awhile to get everything back to the car. He is cold and stiff, and so anxious to get back to a warm room that he nearly forgets his thermos. He walks back down to the dock, eyes scanning the path, trying to figure out just where he put it down last, when he hears an engine again and looks up. It is the car this time, moving across the bridge, but it seems to be in the right lane where the men were working earlier.

He watches, dumbstruck, as the car plows through two wooden barricades and moves with exquisite slowness toward the missing concrete at the top of the bridge. Its front tires go over the edge and turn in the air as if on some invisible surface, and then the front end noses downward. It seems to hang like that for a moment, and then it plunges down into the river.

The force of the fall pushes the vehicle under and for a few seconds it is lost, but then it surfaces again, the open front windows visible just above the surface. The old man is dizzy with the shock of it, but he forces himself to run toward the bank. He is calling, yelling as loudly as he can, though he is not even aware of the words. For one brave, foolish moment he starts into the water, but its numbing cold spills over the tops of his boots and causes him to gulp for air. He backs out and looks around frantically.

Help. He needs to get help. He reaches in his pocket for the phone and then curses to himself when he sees again that he has no service. Then he remembers the public phone he saw up along the main road across from the visitor's center. He noticed it when he came in because you never see those nowadays, everybody having cell phones, but now he understands why. The old man runs toward it, thinking that he must move faster if anyone is to be saved.

Just as his feet reached the smooth asphalt of the road, he is startled by the low rumble of a motor. It is another motorcycle, again coming across the bridge, this one without lights. He freezes, thinking of the broken barricade and the gaping hole in the concrete, but even in the grayness he can see the bike is safely in the left lane. He runs toward it wildly, waving his arms.

The bike slows, and the old man has time only to register a dark shape without features. Much later, he thinks he might have seen a black helmet with a full face shield, but it is nothing he can identify. Then the driver revs the engine and races past him, so close that he can feel the heat of the motorcycle's exhaust. He stands there staring after it, so surprised that he is unable at first to move. Then he looks back at the river and watches as the last edges of the roof rack slide down into the darkness.

He knows that here is no hurry now. Still, the old man runs the last few steps to the phone and dials 911.

Chapter 1

I AM NO ALTRUIST, NOT really. But people call me for help, and I do what I can.

I am advocate, negotiator, counselor, friend. I will get your dog back from your boyfriend after a bad break-up or spend two hours on the phone with your insurance company. I will do what you do not have the time or the stomach to deal with, and you will pay me for it. Gladly.

None of which prepared me for Liz.

It was a Wednesday in March, gray and misty. I had wrapped up my work early and curled up on the settee with a glass of chardonnay and a blanket. As a rule I do not drink before sunset, but something about the chill of day had gotten into my bones. I was immersed in a historical novel, wrapped in a time period four hundred years in the past, only barely aware of the gentle rocking of the boat and the soft slapping of the water against the hull. If you have ever spent any time on a sailboat, you know that feeling of absolute peace that comes from being surrounded by a quiet sea.

Which is why I first ignored the tinny canned ring of my cell phone.

The silence returned, only to be abruptly broken a few seconds later by the same ringtone, though now—and perhaps this was my imagination—it seemed to have caught some sense of the caller's desperation.

I cannot tell you how often I have wondered how differently things might have turned out if I had just not picked up the phone.

"San?"

The voice was muffled and sobbing. I didn't recognize it.

"Yes?"

"It's Liz. You've got to help me. You can't let them put me away."

I was trapped for a moment in mental paralysis. I did not recognize the number on the screen, but the voice was familiar. I had heard it before, sounding almost this way… and then, in a quick flash of memory, it came: Elizabeth Bryson, former co-worker. Liz—a friend once, but we had not spoken in two, maybe three years.

"Liz, what's wrong?"

"I… things have been bad here and Michael, he…he wants to put me away, stick me in an institution. You can't let him… You help people, I know you help people. Please don't let him put me away!"

She was crying, choking; her words were garbled and difficult to distinguish, and my mind was racing to catch up, to fill in the spaces in what she was saying. Liz and I had taught together in the English department at the College of Southern Maryland. She had been young, heavy-set, and fresh from the backwoods of West Virginia, a child of poverty who escaped through the virtue of a high I.Q. and acerbic wit. She met Michael through a friend. He had been twelve years her senior, calm, quiet, stable, and they eloped less than a month later. She was pregnant before the ink dried on the marriage certificate. Then he had received a job offer on the Eastern Shore, and less than a year after little Lizzie's birth, they had gone. There were phone calls at first, then emails, and now the fragile thread of our friendship hung on Facebook posts and hastily written Christmas cards.

"It started because I couldn't stop crying," her voice, stretched high and thin, startled me back to the present. "They had to—had to take me to the emergency room and the doctor said I was dangerous, because Michael said I might hurt the baby, but I wouldn't, you know that, and they gave me shots and wanted to keep me…" Her voice trailed off, and all I could hear was her labored, wet breathing.

"Are you home now? Is Michael there?"

"Michael doesn't want anything to do with me, not after Bernie—" she burst out, then stopped abruptly. There was banging noise, a sound like a door slamming, and a voice in the background. Her voice was low and urgent when she spoke again. "I have to go. Please come and help me. Promise me you won't let them put me away."

It wasn't a rational request. I lived at least six hours and a state away, the weather was miserable, and I hated to drive long distances alone. But something about her tone made me afraid of what she might do. I said yes because I was afraid to say no.

I thought a moment. "Can you hold on until tomorrow morning? I have to cancel an appointment, and it's a long drive in the dark."

"Yes—no—I don't know," she sounded confused, and her voice dropped to a whisper. "Meet me at my house at noon. Please. I knew I could count on you."

The phone went dead.

I sat there staring at it blankly as if it might ring again, or some explanation would appear on the screen. A minute went by, and then two. Nothing happened.

I thought about calling Liz back, but it was obvious that she had needed to get off the phone quickly. I could only guess that she did not want whoever was in the room to know she was talking to me. Without knowing more, I was hesitant to call Liz, and I certainly didn't want to call Michael. The only way I was going to find out what was going on was to go there.

We may think we know the reasons behind our decisions, the logic of our choices, but I have come to understand that much of what we do stems from a few core impulses—love, desire, anger, greed, guilt. This last is more powerful than we think. I know, because I struggle with guilt every day.

Guilt that I did not say "I love you" or "I'm sorry" enough.

Guilt that I am the one left alive.

When I had known Liz, I was a different person. Just turned thirty, happily married, perhaps just a little smug that my life had turned out just the way I expected it to. That changed with a knock on the door at midnight, a police officer standing mute, and the twisted wreckage that littered the interstate. Ryan had been killed on his way home from the airport. He died while I was sleeping.

I fell once, skiing, and had the wind knocked out of me. My husband's death felt exactly like that—it hurt to breathe. The pain dulled me to everything around me. I could not eat, I could not have conversations… I could not function. For a month I alternated between lying in bed and sitting by that same stretch of highway as if it were a memorial. Then, in a sudden frenzy of activity, I sold the house, quit my job, and moved the boat to a little tidewater Virginia town, where I crawled into it like a cocoon. Along the way I severed all human connections as cleanly as if I had cut them with a knife. I called it healing. My mother called it depression.

We were both right.

But suffering takes persistent effort, and after a year of mourning I began to catch myself enjoying things—the taste of the salt air, the pinks in a winter sunset. I took a part-time job covering features for a local magazine, human interest stories about people who were small town heroes, the kind who rescued baby ducks from the middle of Main Street or raised money for soup kitchens. I did not need the money—the settlement from the accident and Ryan's life insurance policy had left me financially secure—but I needed a reason to get up in the morning. I was doing a story on a free medical clinic when I met a woman whose son had been paralyzed in a carnival ride accident. The insurance companies were too busy fighting over which one was the most culpable to actually pay any of the mounting medical bills. I was still smarting from my own run-in with bureaucracy after Ryan's death, which is probably why I made it my mission to become a thorn in the side of every lawyer and ill-named customer service representative involved. It turns out I was good at it.

That is what I do now. Not just insurance problems—any problems. I found that guilt converts very well into righteous anger.

Perhaps I help people because I was not there to help the person I loved most.

It is not something I dwell on anymore.

I made a quick call to reschedule a meeting with a regular client, a landlord with an uncanny knack for choosing deadbeat renters, and checked my contact list for Liz's address. Then I packed an overnight bag and set the alarm for five a.m. Before I fell asleep, I thought that by the time I got to Pineyfield the whole thing would probably have blown over, and it would probably be a wasted trip.

In that, like in so many things that followed, I was mistaken.

Chapter 2

THE DRIVE TO PINEYFIELD THE NEXT morning took six hours and twenty-six minutes, about a half-hour longer than Google Maps predicted thanks to the time I spent sitting in traffic at the Bay Bridge Tunnel. Once across the wide mouth of the Chesapeake, the road became empty and the scenery shifted to flat brown fields that stretched on either side of the highway. It was another chilly, overcast day, with no line separating earth from sky. I found myself wondering what Ryan had felt, face down on the cold asphalt, in the moments before he died. It was not an uplifting thought, and I turned up the radio to make it go away.

I entered the town of Pineyfield just after I crossed the Virginia/Maryland line, and it was as uninspiring as its name suggested. The welcome sign was chipped and faded and several of the sponsoring organizations seemed to have peeled off altogether. I wasn't sure where to go from here—my cell signal disappeared upon arrival, making my mapping app suddenly worthless. There were no 7-Elevens or McDonald's to be seen, squelching any hope I had of picking up WiFi. The few identifiable businesses were in houses or converted metal sheds, including the Pineyfield Grocery Mart just ahead of me (which fell under the shed category). I pulled into the gravel lot, narrowly avoided a pothole, and parked by a bucket full of cigarette butts.

Inside a weathered, heavyset older man was behind the single counter listening to a police scanner. A large jar of pickled pigs' feet to his right caught and held my eyes, so that a minute or two passed before I remembered why I was there.

"Excuse me. Could you tell me how to get to Osprey Drive?" I asked, smiling as warmly as I could endeavor.

He just looked at me.

"I'm looking for a friend," I explained, shifting my feet under his silent scrutiny. "I need to find Elizabeth Bryson's house. It's at 42 Osprey Drive. Could you help me?"

The man opened his mouth and yawned, revealing several gaping holes where there should have been teeth. Then he shook his head sadly.

"'Scuse me. Been a slow mornin'. Yer on about that teacher, I reckon. It's a cryin' shame. A young feller like that and three little ones. Now how do you figger it happened?" he asked, peering at me closely.

"I really can't say," I faltered.

"Guess you can't," he agreed, nodding, as if this confirmed some unspoken suspicion about outsiders.

"Do you know how to get to Osprey Drive?" I asked, after he did not seem inclined to say more.

"Course I do. Lived here all my life," he said with a trace of indignation. "Down the road a piece, cut 'er left at the fillin' station, go a ways past the chicken farm, and you'll see 'er on the right. Bayview."

I only caught a part of what he said, but since he seemed to get less intelligible the longer he spoke, I didn't think it would do much good to ask him to repeat them. I thanked him, got in my car, and spent the next half-hour being lost before finally getting directions from a dirty-faced twelve-year-old who only agreed to talk to me after I assured him I was not a truancy officer.

My first sight of the Bryson residence was something of a surprise. It was in one of those sad little subdivisions plunked in the middle of a treeless field and consisted of three dozen or more vinyl-sided boxes on little quarter-acre squares. It looked as if it once had visions of becoming upscale, with a brick pillars and wrought iron street posts that all bore the names of water fowl, but there was absolutely no bay—not even a marsh—in evidence. Michael and Liz both were well-educated and had good jobs. It is true that no neighborhood looks its best in March, but this didn't seem like a place either of them would belong.

42 Osprey Drive was a gray rambler with black shutters and a small front porch. A few scraggly bushes lined the sidewalk up to the door, and two hanging baskets on either side of the front door were empty. I pulled in behind the silver minivan parked in the driveway. I counted three car seats as I walked by.

My palms were sweating as I climbed the front steps. I heard wailing as I rang the bell, and then the front door was opened a few feet by a pretty child of about five.

"How may I help you?" she asked seriously.

I fell in love with her instantly. I am not particularly comfortable around children, but I have a weakness for the precocious miniature adult. This must have been Lizzie, whom I remembered only as a round-faced cherub on her mother's lap.

"I'm Ms. Beck. Is your mommy at home?"

She shook her head, her small face holding a thousand secrets and giving none away.

"What about your daddy?"

Lizzie nodded and opened the door more widely. Then she took my hand and led me into the living room just as her father entered from the kitchen, a toddler clinging to one knee and an infant on his shoulder.

"You must be from the coroner's office," he said, without even the shadow of a smile.

Michael Bryson was forty-five, and he looked it. He was thin, with longish salt and pepper hair and a sensitive face that was lined around the eyes and mouth. He wore jeans and an old blue sweater. I had met him only a few times before, and back then he had been short-haired and stiffly attired, looking every inch the CPA. If I saw him in a coffee shop now, I would have pegged him as a college professor or perhaps an artist. A cold tingling crawled up the back of my neck. "No. I know you don't remember me, Michael, but I'm Sandra Beck, a friend of Liz's. Is she here?"

.Michael Bryson juggled the infant around and stared at me. The pause was so long that I repeated myself.

"I know who you are," he said without expression. "You better sit down."

I cleared away a Barbie doll and a See and Spell and sat on the couch. I had already taken in the room: beachy pillows in pastel colors, scented candles, and discount family portraits in seashell frames. I couldn't imagine Liz—all bright colors and sharp angles, with a flair for the dramatic—living in this soft, ordinary house.

"I didn't recognize you. It's been a long time," Michael said, clearing his throat. "Lizzie, could I talk to Mrs. Beck alone for just a minute?"

The child nodded gravely and left the room. Michael turned back to me.

"I don't know how to say this. I wasn't expecting to have to tell anyone else."

"Did you have Liz institutionalized?" I asked sharply.

Directness is only one of my flaws, but it has proven useful more than once.

Michael pressed his lips together and looked away from me. There was a long, uncomfortable silence, which gave me more than enough time to consider that in this instance perhaps I should not have opened my mouth. Finally, he brushed his hand over his eyes and then looked straight at me. They were dark with tears.

"I don't know why you would say that, or what you've heard, but you're wrong. Elizabeth was killed in a car accident last night."

I am not proud of what happened next. There was a buzzing in my ears, and perspiration broke out on my forehead. The same words, the crush of memory—*killed*—*a car accident*—and the walls closed in around me. My body loosened like liquid and my vision narrowed to blackness.

From what seemed like a great distance I heard Michael get up and the cry of the baby, and then someone shook my shoulder, and I felt a glass of water against my lips. I managed to curl my hand around it and take several sips before my eyes cleared. Michael's face leaned over me, forehead creased with worry.

"I'm sorry. That was really thoughtless of me....I shouldn't have told you like that. I forgot about your husband," he said. "Are you all right?"

I nodded, and he slid back into his chair, absently patting the back of the wailing infant lying across his shoulder. The toddler was sitting on the floor in front of me, watching me with undisguised interest.

"I'm sorry. I didn't know," I whispered.

Michael didn't respond, but continued to pat the back of the baby as it rubbed its wet face on his shirt.

"She—she called me yesterday. That's why I thought…"

He went still. "What time?"

"Around four-thirty." I hesitated. "She asked me… to come. She wanted me to meet her here at twelve."

Michael's voice was edged with some emotion I could not place.

"Did she say why?"

I didn't know if he meant why she had called, or why she wanted me, and I did not know how to answer either question. Just then, perhaps sensing the tension in the room, the toddler began to cry, his lower sobs blending discordantly with the high-pitched wail of the baby. Michael called to Lizzie, who had been waiting like a silent sentry just around the corner.

"Could you take Joshua back to his room and play with him for a little while?"

The child nodded, and as soon as she put out her hand the boy stopped crying. She took his small fist gently and led him down a short hallway and out of my sight.

At that moment the phone rang. Michael excused himself and went into the kitchen, still holding the fussing baby. Over the noise, I could still hear his voice clearly through the thin walls.

"Bill, hi...No, it's all right. I appreciate all you've done... listen, I've got an old friend of Liz's here who says Liz talked to her around four-thirty yesterday afternoon... yes, I told her... no... I thought you might. Should she stay here? No., but thanks, I appreciate it. We're hanging in there. Tell your wife thank you for this morning....Right. Goodbye."

When he came back into the room the baby was cradled in his arm, sucking loudly on a bottle.

"That was Deputy Wathen. From what you say, you were the last person to talk to Liz. He would like to talk to you. He said he had just a few questions."

This didn't make sense to me. No one had cared who Ryan talked to before he had been killed or what they had said.

"I don't—" I started, but he held up his hand to stop me.

"Bill—Deputy Wathen—said we shouldn't talk about it until he talked to you. He said he'd appreciate it if you'd come to the station."

The news of Liz's death had already left me shaken, and I was not sure I could handle talking to the police. I felt like I needed to process everything, but Michael was already walking to the door.

"Can you at least tell me what kind of accident—"

He shook his head, cutting off all further conversation.

I rose and followed him. He opened the door without speaking, his expression steeped in a bottomless sadness I knew too well. Without thinking, I reached out my hand and touched his arm.

Michael Bryson began to cry, long soft gulps, tears falling on the downy head of the baby he held. I stood for a moment, uncertain. Then I felt a gentle tug on my jacket. It was Lizzie, standing beside me, her face solemn.

"Goodbye," she said softly.

I flushed as if I had been caught at something and dropped my hand. Michael walked away slowly, his back to me, and Lizzie pushed open the front door. I stepped out and the door closed softly behind me.

I stood there blankly. I don't know how many minutes passed before I became aware of the cold dampness of the day against my skin. I shook my head as if that action could order my thoughts and got in my car.

The loud roar of the motor seemed almost comforting against the heavy quiet that hung on this place. As I backed from the driveway, I caught the movement of a curtain at one of the bedroom windows.

The last thing I saw in the pale spring light was the face of the dead woman's five-year-old daughter pressed against the glass.

Chapter 3

I DROVE BACK TOWARD THE town. Now, in place of the empty blankness, my thoughts were a chaotic jumble. It was like listening to ten songs at one time. I could tune nothing out, and over it all *Liz is dead Liz is dead Liz is dead* played itself crazily like the rounds we used to sing as children. I must have driven four or five miles and passed the turn I came in on when I realized I had no idea where I was going.

There were a few trailers with pick-up trucks and an occasional farmhouse, but no other signs of development. I made a concerted effort to still the voices in my head, did a U-turn, and drove back in what I hoped to be the direction of downtown Pineyfield.

I had just passed the grocery store when I spotted a small wooden sign that pointed in the direction of what was optimistically labeled the "Town Center." I turned left on Main Street, a tree-lined boulevard with a dozen or so older homes lining the cracked sidewalk. I passed a thrift store, a barber shop, and several empty storefronts. A few elderly people were out walking dogs, and one grizzled gentleman was smoking a cigar, seemingly unaware that his jacket was unevenly buttoned and hanging at an angle. There were a few benches, and small banners hung from the streetlamps proclaiming "Pineyfield—100 Years," the signs of an unsuccessful renewal project. At the far end of the street stood a long, nondescript two-story brick building with few windows, a flagpole, and a large paved parking lot. According to the sign, it housed everything from the school board to the unemployment office to the local jail. The sheriff's department was in suite 101.

The lobby was small and empty, but the noise of voices and the ringing of phones drifted in from the open door at the end of the hall. I walked back to find suite 101 consisted of a waiting area, a glassed-in counter, and two or three cubicles walled off by bright orange dividers. From the entrance I could see a uniformed officer interviewing a woman in the first cubicle. She had a black eye and runny nose, and she stopped periodically to cry into a wad of tissues that she fished out of the pocket of the oversized camouflage jacket she wore. No one was at the counter, so I sat in one of the vinyl chairs and waited.

"Mariellen, if you don't file the charges, there's nothin' I can do," the officer said in a pleading tone. "It'll just happen again."

"He says he's sorry."

"Mariellen, he's always sorry until the next time he gets drunk. You'd be doin' him a favor."

She shook her head stubbornly and continued to cry. The officer pushed his chair back in exasperation.

"Then there's nothin' I can do. You might as well go on home."

This was apparently not what Mariellen wanted either, because she pushed past him in some anger, tears momentarily forgotten.

"Nothin' is all you ever do. None of you is any damn good!"

She stalked down the hallway, and the officer looked after her, shaking his head. He was young, perhaps twenty-five, with short, light hair and wire-rimmed glasses. He had a pleasant face, the sort you'd be comforted to see at two in the morning when your alarm went off. Not, I'm sure, that anyone in Pineyfield had an alarm. No, I'm sure they all had shotguns instead.

He caught sight of me then and started.

"I'm sorry, ma'am, I didn't see you there," he said, putting on a smile. "Can I help you?"

I stood up and extended my hand. I had to clear my throat before I could speak.

"I hope so. I'm Sandi Beck. Michael Bryson said a Deputy Wathen wanted to see me."

"Damn shame." He shook his head, the smile gone. "I'm Deputy Wathen," he added as he placed one hand beneath my elbow and steered me into his cubicle.

He moved behind his desk and flopped down with a sigh that seemed to come out as "All righty then." He swung around in his chair and pulled two soda cans from a small refrigerator behind his desk. He handed one to me, studying my face as if trying to place it. "Coke?"

I was suddenly aware of a savage thirst. I thanked him and reached for the can, realizing as I did that my hand was shaking. He noticed it, too, his eyes flicking down and then back to my face. He waited while I pulled the tab, then opened his own can. He raised it to me in a mock toast. We drank in silence for a moment, and then he put his can on the desk and leaned forward.

"I don't know how much help you can be, but it sounds like you're the last person to talk to her," Deputy Wathen said, and he made it sound like he wasn't sure that was a good thing. "Now, I know this might be hard, but I'm gonna' ask a few questions. You don't have to answer right away. You can think on 'em a minute. All righty?"

I nodded.

"Where are you from?"

"I live near Irvington, Virginia," I answered, and then seeing his blank look, I added, "It's a little town near Kilmarnock on the western short of the Bay."

"That's a right long piece to drive. And what do you do over there in Irvington?"

"I am a personal advocacy consultant."

Walthen raised an eyebrow. "Can't say as I've ever hear of a personal advocacy consultant. What kind of job is that, exactly?"

It is a question I am used to hearing. "I try to iron out problems in situations that involve insurance companies or broken contracts, that sort of thing."

He looked at me curiously. "Like a lawyer, then?"

"No. I just—I do what most people don't have time to do on their own. I do research, I make calls, I write letters."

"And does that pay well?"

I couldn't see how this related to Liz's death. I frowned.

"Well enough."

The deputy caught the hint.

"So then, you came over this morning, is that right?"

I nodded.

"Were you comin' over to the beach for business, for a vacation, or because of Liz's call?"

I knew that "the beach" was the resort town of Ocean City, a popular spot for conventions in the off-season. It was less than a forty-five minute drive away, but for some reason none of its economic success had trickled down to Pineyfield.

"Her call."

He nodded, as if the answers thus far fit his expectations.

"Did you all talk often?"

"I hadn't talked to Liz for probably three years before last night."

The deputy raised his eyebrows.

"Did you all write regular?"

"No... a Christmas card, you know... birth announcement... that kind of thing."

Deputy Wathen leaned forward, his brow crinkled. "You don't hear from her for three years and then when she calls, you drive three hundred miles just like that. Now, she must have said something powerful to get that kind of reaction, wouldn't you say?"

I looked at him, and I knew.

I didn't answer.

"What did she say to you, Miz Beck? Was she lookin' to have you iron out something for her over here?"

Nervousness squeezed at my intestines. Something was wrong with all of this. I remembered the police after Ryan's accident... no questions, just averted faces, soft words...

"You don't think Liz's death was an accident, do you, Deputy?"

He leaned back in his chair, and took a long, slow drag on his soda.

"Why would you ask that, Miz Beck?"

"Because I'm here for questioning. You don't ask questions about an accident to someone who was 300 miles away when it happened."

"Then let's get down to it," the deputy said, looking at me directly. "Do you have any reason for thinking Elizabeth Bryson might want to harm herself? Anything she said on the phone?"

"You think she killed herself?"

"What I think," the deputy said in a measured tone, "doesn't matter a damn bit. I have a car that ran off a bridge and a victim who is presumed dead. I have a phone call so urgent that a woman drives what—five, six hours?—to see someone she hasn't talked to in three years. What I have to do is find out whether the one has any bearing on the other."

"Presumed dead?" The wording surprised me. "You didn't find her body?"

"I'll tell you what, Miz Beck, you answer my question, and then I'll answer yours."

It felt like betrayal.

"She was upset when she called. She was crying," I said, somewhat reluctantly.

"Did she say why?"

"No, not really," I lied. I felt that I was protecting someone, but I could not say who. Perhaps the sad-eyed child.

"And did she ask you to come here today? Or last night?"

"She asked me to come as soon as I could. I told her I'd drive here this morning. Why would she-" I began.

"Why would she kill herself if she had asked you to come here? I don't know, Miz Beck. People do strange things."

"What makes you think it's a suicide? Did she leave a note?" I asked.

"No, she did not, and I am not sure of anything. Officially, it's an accident, and that's how I hope to leave it," Bill Wathen said with an air of finality. "None of us wants to see Michael Bryson lose the insurance money or have to tell his little girl that her momma ran her car off a bridge on purpose. I just want to know from you that nothing is going to come up later on that would end up givin' me or anyone else here a heartache."

I struggled. What if that call had been, not a cry for help, but a cry for vindication? A last message to Michael, or the man she called Bernie, or the sad-eyed child? Was I supposed to be Elizabeth Bryson's living suicide note?

That was a responsibility I did not want. I made a decision.

"No. There was nothing like that. She said she had been depressed, and she wanted to see me. I gathered she and Michael were having some problems. That was really about all. Nothing to suggest she was planning to take her own life."

He nodded, and the tension between us eased. "All righty then. Let me tell you what happened. I was the officer on the scene. I'm the only officer in town right now, with Buddy and Pete on vacation. I got the call around 5:40 p.m. A tourist on the emergency phone outside of the national park office over at Assateague. That's about, oh, fifteen, twenty minutes from here. He's all shook up, says he saw a car go off the bridge. It was under construction, a big section missin' on one lane, and it just went right through the barriers. Well, he called 911, and they routed him here. I was already over that way, so it only took me five or ten minutes to get there. I called the Coast Guard patrol in Ocean City, and the Fire Department in Snow Hill—that's closer to the bridge than Pineyfield—while I was headed over there. By then, her husband had called the school because she was late comin' home, and when they told him she left around four-thirty, I guess he got worried and called the sheriff's department. With what he said and Mr. Strauss's description of the car, we had a pretty good idea who we were lookin' for, but the tide was just runnin' out, and it took nearly two hours to pull up the car. It had gone right in the channel, and the current had started to drag it to the mouth of the bay. Another hour and it would have been in the Atlantic." He paused to take a drink.

"What about her body?"

Deputy Wathen shook his head. "No, but that's no real surprise. If she got out in the water, she's light enough that she'd have been dragged out to sea pretty quick—that current can run as much as five knots."

"You knew Elizabeth Bryson?"

He seemed to start a bit, and he threw me a suddenly guarded look. "What do you mean?"

"You said she was light enough. I just wondered if you knew her."

The deputy seemed to relax a little. "Her weight and all were in the report, but, yeah, I knew Liz. Leastways, I knew who she was. Pineyfield's a small town. Plus, my older brother Bernie's the vice-principal at the school where she worked, and he's mentioned her too."

Bernie. What had she said? Right after the part about Michael not wanting anything to do with her, "not after Bernie."

"She mentioned your brother when she called. Was she... having some problems at work?" I asked.

Color suffused the deputy's face.

"I don't know anything about Liz's work performance, Miz Beck. He just mentioned her job in passin'."

I looked at my lap. He could never have played poker. The suddenly cold tone and the flushed face were a clear admission of guilt. But whose? Bernie's? With Liz?

I looked up to find Deputy Wathen staring at me. I shook my head.

"I'm sorry. This has all been... something of a shock... I wish I could understand...." I paused and shrugged, at a loss for words.

Deputy Wathen nodded, once again all sympathy. "Yeah, I guess it must have been. I'm real sorry."

"The man who reported her car going off the bridge... did he say it looked deliberate?"

He opened a desk drawer and shuffled through some files, pulling one out and handing it to me. "No. Couldn't say one way or the other. That's the eyewitness account given by Mr. Strauss, the fisherman from Baltimore.

He's renting a place at the beach for a month. His address is there. was trying to get a copy of the off road vehicle regulations. He bought some old truck for fishing, but the visitor's center closes at five in the off-season. He was on his way back out when he heard the noise. One lane of the bridge was closed off—a ten-foot section of the bridge and the cement side wall had been removed for structural repairs. Car ran over two cones and then went through the wooden barricade. That's what caught his attention. He looked up just about when it hit the water, so he didn't see if anything made her go in."

"Did he try to find her?"

"After he called, and I gather that took a few minutes. No cell towers there at all, so he couldn't get any reception. Had to use the park's emergency phone in the parking lot across the street. Then he ran up and down the bank, lookin'—said he'd have gone in if he had seen anything, but that water's too damn cold, and he's seventy years old. If he'd tried, they'd have both been dead."

"So he never saw a body?"

The deputy shook his head. "No. He did flag down another vehicle—a man on a motorcycle, before I got there—but the guy wouldn't stop. You can't really blame him. Gettin' dark, deserted area, and this Strauss is running down the street wavin' his arms."

I thought about this. I'd been to the same park several times over summer vacations. "Isn't there just one main road into that area?"

"Yes ma'am."

"Did you pass the motorcyclist when you were going in?"

Deputy Wathen fiddled with his glasses a minute, pushing them up and down the bridge of his nose.

"Not that I recall—but then, I wasn't looking," he said matter-of-factly. "Still, I can't see as how it would make much difference. Fella's not likely to have seen it since it had happened five or ten minutes beforehand."

That was true, and I didn't see how it would make a difference either. I don't know what I was trying to prove, only that I felt the responsibility of having talked to Liz in the hour before her death. I wanted someone to blame, or at least, to absolve me.

"I just don't understand. Why would Liz have been going across that bridge at five-thirty at night? It's not on the way to anywhere but the park, and you said that was closed."

He avoided my eyes. "Well, ma'am, I can't say as I know. Now then, I thank you for coming down, If you'll just jot down a number I can reach

;e comes up, you can be on your way." I filled out the
the desk. Then he rose and motioned for the door. "I
to head back home."
:red before I had even realized that I had made up my
there will be some kind of memorial service. I'll stay for

He looked as if this news did not agree with him.

"They were Catholics, you know. The priest from Ocean City is working something up, but it won't be until Saturday. "

"That's only two days. It's not a problem," I replied.

Deputy Wathen nodded his thanks and walked me to the front door.

"You know," he said, looking carefully at me, "sometimes there is no real answer. In this job, I see people hurt in all kinds of ways. There isn't always a reason why."

I nodded and shook the proffered hand. I had learned this lesson, too, but there was no comfort in it. In the weeks after Ryan's death, I had succumbed to my own private madness. Sometimes I had gone in the morning, or in the afternoon rush hour. Twice I had awakened from a fitful sleep and raced there, driven by a force stronger than reason. I had haunted that stretch of interstate where Ryan had bled and died more persistently than any spirit, watching the cars, wondering why not this one, why not that one, why him. The only answer I had ever come up with was that there was no answer. Gradually, the madness faded to resignation and a bleak despair. My God, if I had one at all, was a God of only rough justice.

I drove to Ocean City, some twenty-five miles away. A long bridge separated this barrier island from the mainland, and crossing it was like entering a different country. The mainland lay flat and brown, forests of scrub pine broken only by farmhouses, truck-stop towns, and, near the bridge, cheap rental cottages. From this wasteland the bridge rose like Jacob's Ladder, leading into a steel and concrete heaven of high rise hotels, health clubs, boutiques and restaurants. Now, in the off-season, the streets were deserted and most of the shops had boarded windows with signs announcing upcoming openings in May. I found a hotel advertising reduced rates, a heated pool, and continental breakfast far from any place that Ryan and I had stayed.

I had fallen into this habit subconsciously. Since his death, I had frequented different stores, eaten at different restaurants, walked different stretches of beach. It was protection against the merciless waves of memory that had once threatened to pin me under and suffocate me. I was better, yes—but I was still not whole.

I checked in and carried my single bag up to the seventh floor. I would have to go shopping for other clothes if I really intended to stay here, but I was exhausted. I took a hot shower and lay on the bed in front of the sliding glass door of the beach front hotel, staring at the cold silver ocean. I felt the day loosen and slip from me like molting skin. I let the beach enfold me. In March it is like the surface of the moon, barren and white. and the wind blows relentlessly. It is a seductive wildness.

I thought about Liz. Drowning has never seemed a terrible way to die to me. I could imagine the water embracing her like the arms of a mother, soothing away her worry, carrying her into a death that was empty of pain.

Is that how she had imagined it as well?

Just below the surface was the fact that Elizabeth Bryson had been an unhappy woman. I did not need the memory of her sobbing voice to confirm this. It had been in the eyes of her husband, of the deputy, and even in the eyes of the five-year-old child. Something worse than discontent and dirty diapers. Something more than a failure of the brakes, a skid off of a guardrail. I knew that I had already made a judgement. I believed Liz had ended her own life purposely. But did it matter? Was it really any of my business, a friend who was so distant as to know only scraps and pieces of her life? I had come to help, but there was no longer any help to give. Besides, my duty, if I had any based on the phone call, was to the living, to those left behind.

I was interrupted in this reverie by the ring of my cell phone. An unknown caller. I picked up and was answered by a man's voice, unfamiliar to me. I was surprised when he identified himself as Bernie Wathen.

"My brother told me that you talked to Liz, Miss Beck."

His tone was curt, authoritative, and accusing. I felt a flash of guilt—for what?—followed by extreme irritation.

"It's Mrs. Beck, Mr. Wathen."

There was a slight pause. "I'm sorry?"

One advantage to my recent work experience was a honed ability to control unpleasant phone conversations. I used the clipped, controlled voice that I normally unleashed on insurance adjusters.

"Mrs. It is my title. I am a widow, and I prefer to be addressed correctly."

I must have ruined his timing because he seemed to be having trouble working up to his original tone. I didn't give him a chance.

"Did you want something?" I asked brusquely.

There was a pause. When he finally spoke, he actually sounded humble. "I'd like to see you for a few minutes if I could. I need to talk to you about Elizabeth."

"I had planned on attending the memorial service, Mr. Wathen," I said discouragingly.

"No. Please. I'd prefer to meet privately. It... it really is important."

Intrigued in spite of myself, I agreed to meet him in the hotel lounge in half an hour.

I suspected that Liz had been having an affair with Bernie Wathen. Why else would she have mentioned him? Why else would the deputy have treated their relationship so carefully? Pineyfield was a small town, and there had probably been plenty of talk already. Bernie's brother would have called him as soon as I left to tell him that Liz had mentioned him in her last conversation. He had to be wondering how much she had told me. Perhaps Deputy Wathen and his brother were afraid that I would spread that story.

If Liz's death were ruled an accident, whatever secrets she and Bernie held between them died on the Assateague Bridge. There might be rumors, but these would fade in the absence of any new material. But if someone started to question whether Liz had purposely driven off of that bridge, attention would turn to every unhappy aspect of her life. It would be scrutinized, not just by the police or insurance investigators, but over every breakfast table and next to every hometown office coffee pot. Was she unstable? Was the husband cruel or abusive? Was there a lover? In a small town, these were questions I thought Bernie Wathen would not want answered.

Chapter 4

AS SOON AS I SAW IT, I realized the lounge had been a poor choice for a meeting.

The hotel had obviously been going for a tropical feel. The area designated as the lounge was really a large atrium that included an indoor heated swimming pool, some rattan furniture, and a bar with an aquarium in the front. Everything was separated by huge potted palm trees and bright flowers, but the chlorine smell from the pool was overwhelming, and the air seemed permanently warm and moist, like a men's locker room. It was relatively uncrowded. A small group of children screamed and splashed by the pool, their fathers at the bar holding towels and watching ESPN, and Bernie Wathen—who else could it be?—standing on the side, looking uncomfortably hot in a navy blue polyester suit and tie.

I walked over and extended my hand with a confidence I did not feel.

"Mr. Wathen, I'm Sandra Beck."

He eyed me suspiciously. "I see you didn't have any trouble picking me out of the crowd."

I wasn't sure if this was an attempt at humor, so I smiled slightly. "Well, it isn't very crowded in the off-season, is it?"

He didn't answer, but looked around me as if expecting another Mrs. Beck to emerge from the palm grove. There was a long pause while sweat beads formed and rolled off of his forehead.

"Mr. Wathen, you wanted to talk to me?" I prompted.

He finally focused on my face.

"I, uh... well." His eyes darted around the atrium, then back to me, focusing somewhere off my left shoulder. "There's a place just down the block that's quiet."

I wasn't too thrilled about going anywhere with Bernie Wathen, but it was obvious that he would pass out if we stayed in the atrium.

"All right. You say it's close. Should we drive or walk?"

He looked at me in surprise. "Too cold to walk. I'll drive."

He turned his back to me and started for the exit. I took a few long strides and fell in step beside him, taking this opportunity to focus on his appearance. I do not habitually look at men. Since Ryan's death, they have become an undiscovered country I choose not to enter. But earlier today I found myself staring at Michael Bryson, and now I was staring at Bernie Wathen: the two men in Liz's life.

My first thought was that they couldn't have been more different. Bernie was a large man with a florid face, large ears, and a bad haircut. Several extra inches squeezed out over his belt, and he looked like twenty minutes on a Stairmaster might kill him. I just couldn't imagine Liz Bryson making love with this man.

For his part, Wathen neither spoke nor looked my way, not even when we climbed inside his big Buick. He did not seem to notice when I had to kick aside a pile of wrappers and empty chip bags to make room for my feet on the passenger floor. He drove in silence for a few blocks and pulled into a long driveway that ended back on the bayside at a red neon sign that said "Mike's." It was a one-room local dive with a tattered awning and an empty parking lot. The inside was about what you would expect: standard stained tile, Formica booths, pool table, juke box, peeling paint on the ceiling, metal stool at the bar. We were the only customers. The bartender was absently wiping the counter and humming to classic rock when we came in.

"Hey, Bernie, how's it hangin'?"

Bernie nodded and led me to a booth at the shadowed corner, putting my back to the door. He was tense.

"Beer?" he asked shortly, looking past me as if watching for someone.

I was tempted to ask for a nice cabernet just to see his expression. Unfortunately, if I ordered wine, I just might get it, and I suspected that anything they served here would come from a box with a plastic spout. I said that a beer sounded fine. Bernie motioned to the bartender in what must have been some universal signal, and two drafts appeared on the table.

"So what were you getting at with my brother?"

He was trying to sound unconcerned, but the sweat stood out on his upper lip, and he was systematically tearing at the skin around his fingernails—first one hand, then the other.

"Mr. Wathen, I wasn't getting at anything. All I said was that Liz mentioned you on the phone. She did," I emphasized.

The words hung for a moment between us.

Bernie nodded once, more to himself than to me. Then he rose and took off his jacket, rolling up his shirtsleeves. When he sat back down, he tried to sound relaxed and friendly, though I noticed he kept his hands in his lap.

"Sandi," he said, in a country drawl that was more pronounced now, "you don't mind if I call you Sandi, do you? I don't mind tellin' you I am takin' Liz's death hard. We all are. But that doesn't change what happened."

There was a kind of eager slipperiness in his voice, like a used car salesman about to close a deal. I looked down, avoiding eye contact, and found myself staring at an orange and black tattoo hidden beneath the dense hair of his forearm.

"And what did happen?"

"Now I don't mean any disrespect, Sandi, but isn't it obvious that she lost control of her car, went off that bridge, and drowned? Someone saw her go in, and they've pulled her car. My brother wrote it up as accidental death. Now he got the impression from you that you're going to make trouble, start a rumor that it wasn't an accident."

"Look, Bernie." I leaned heavily on his name in retaliation for his familiarity. "I'm not from here, don't know anyone over here, so I don't know who you or your brother think I would tell even if I did believe that Liz's death was intentional."

He nodded and opened his mouth, but I wasn't finished.

"The thing is, I grew up in Maryland. I've come here for vacations most of my life and I've driven that bridge a dozen times myself. To be perfectly honest, it is hard to see why Liz would have even been there, or how she could have accidentally driven off that bridge."

He picked up his beer, then put it down again and looked away. His face was flushed and his voice had the faintest hint of a quaver.

"You want to call it suicide, is that it?"

"I don't want to call it anything. I want to know what really happened."

Bernie snorted derisively. He raised his voice and it took on a rough edge.

"The truth is she's dead, and draggin' the rest of us through the mud won't help anybody but the insurance company! Are you going to put everyone through that to save some CEO a few bucks?"

He had nearly shouted. The bartender shot him a warning look, and Bernie fell silent, sipping his beer sulkily.

I didn't like Bernie Wathen, and I didn't trust him. But he was right about one thing—Liz was dead. What difference could it possibly make to dissect her motives or unearth her demons? I remembered that sad little face pressed against the glass, and suddenly I wanted to cry.

"You don't understand. I want it to be an accident. I do. I'm just afraid that it wasn't, and I feel like maybe I should have done something." As soon as I said it, I knew it was true. I felt as if I had exposed a raw wound to salt air, and it stung.

The admission struck a chord in the man across from me. He softened and crumbled as two tears welled up and trailed fat drops down his cheeks. He wiped them away with his bar napkin.

"If it's anybody's fault, it's mine."

He cried quietly for a few minutes. I waited in awkward silence for him to go on.

"We... we were involved, Liz and me. I think you already knew that."

He looked up at me, but I didn't say anything. He looked down again and went on.

"I'm married... but me and my wife, we've been havin' problems. I worked late a lot, and Liz was, well, she was lonely, and depressed, and it… it just happened. I never meant for it to go anywhere. My wife... she doesn't know."

He looked up at me, waiting. Now that the dam had broken, he wanted to talk to purge his soul.

"How long had you been seeing each other?" I asked.

Bernie wiped his eyes again on his cocktail napkin, then his nose, and sniffled.

"Since before Christmas... maybe November, thereabouts."

"Did Michael Bryson know?"

He thought about this for a moment, then shook his head.

"I don't think so. I hope to hell he didn't. I wouldn't want him to—to remember her like that."

Neither would I. Perhaps I had misunderstood what she had said on the phone.

"When was the last time you saw Liz?"

Bernie moved in his seat uncomfortably. "That day. At school."

"Did you see her alone after school?"

He nodded, and I pressed on.

"Did something happen between the two of you that day?"

I could see him regaining control and regretting the loss of his guard. "I... I told her I couldn't see her anymore. My wife was starting to hear things. This is a small community. I couldn't take the chance."

"How did she react?"

"She was upset, you know, cryin' and everything. But I figured that was normal, you know, she'd get over it. She said she was going to take a drive, think things over, and I said that was a good idea. We both left school right around four-thirty. The next thing I knew was when Bill called me around seven-thirty or so at home. That was right after they found the car, but he was pretty sure... you know."

I was starting to dislike Bernie Wathen all over again. I hated the way he was dancing around the whole thing, as if it had been a bad meal or an embarrassing slip of the tongue, better to be glossed over and quickly forgotten.

"That she was dead," I said bluntly.

"Yes," he said and looked chastened.

"Do you believe that Liz purposely took her own life?"

He reached across the table and put his hand on my arm. He looked in my eyes with practiced sincerity, once again the gentleman, his voice pitched comfortingly.

"Sandi, you asked me what I believe. I believe that with the construction, that bridge was dangerous. I believe it was near evening. I believe Liz could have been cryin', or she could have been sick. I believe none of us will ever know for certain what happened on that bridge, but I believe Liz's children do not need to grow up believin' their mother killed herself."

Up until this moment, I could not have told you what Liz could possibly have seen in this man. But the soft, steady pressure on my arm, and the intensity of his gaze... I could picture her, sitting at her desk, weary of the tears and the pastel wallpaper and the diapers, and then him, leaning over her, his smell lacing the air—the smell of Old Spice, of tobacco, of fathers and uncles and solid men, men you could depend on.

"I have to go," I said abruptly, moving beyond his reach.

Bernie sat back, a little surprised.

"You're done? You didn't finish your beer."

"I don't feel well. I think it has all been so sudden, and it's just now sinking in, if you know what I mean. It was," I groped for the polite phrase," it was nice meeting you, Bernie."

"You're still comin' to the memorial service?" he asked, rising with me.

"I... I don't know."

He nodded and seemed satisfied.

"I'll give you a ride back to the hotel."

"No," I said quickly. "That's all right. I need the exercise."

"Are you sure? It's only about fifty degrees out, and it's damp—"

"I'm sure." The walls were closing in, and I hurried to the door. "Thanks anyway. Thanks for the beer. Goodbye."

I left Bernie looking perplexed and escaped into the cold, wet air.

I did not go straight back to the hotel. Instead, I crossed Ocean Highway and headed for the beach. By this time it was late afternoon and the sky was deepening to a dark steel gray. The air was so heavy with moisture that I felt as if I were walking through clouds. I wanted to say that to someone, *It feels like walking through clouds*, but there was no one. Would I ever get used to this, this impulse to talk to Ryan? Every feeling, every flash of an idea we had told each other. Without anyone to tell, my thoughts did not even seem real. It was like the old adage about the tree falling in the forest. Without anyone to hear, I no longer even knew if I was falling.

It wasn't only talking. It was touching. Not just sex—although God knows that had been great. Ryan and I had been constantly physical in our affection for each other, but very separate from everyone else around us. We touched constantly—in the car, at the dinner table, in our sleep—but we seldom hugged friends or acquaintances. It was as if we had reserved our bodies for each other. Immediately following Ryan's death I had been inundated with the sympathetic embraces of everyone who knew me. I had very nearly drowned in a sea of hugs and kisses, squeezes and pats. When I regained my sense of self, I gradually sealed off my skin from the touch of all others. I don't know how many well-meaning people I hurt in the process. I didn't care. Now I think that I subconsciously tried to enclose my body in glass, to preserve it, so that no physical sensation replaced my memory of Ryan's touch. In the past three years, I had managed to close myself off from all of the contact which makes us human.

That had to be why it still felt warm where Bernie touched my arm.

I was so engrossed in thought I barely noticed I had reached the beach. I slipped off my shoes and stepped onto the cold sand, shadowed by the concrete and glass giants behind me. The breeze had died, and the ocean barely spoke as it curled on to the shore. I looked out to the fading eastern horizon. Was Liz's body out there somewhere, carried by the tide and floating beneath the cold silver surface? At least I had seen Ryan's body. Michael had nothing. An empty car. A vague and impossible hope.

If I felt somehow responsible, how must he feel? If Liz had taken her own life, then he had been right to try to get help for her. Did he blame himself for not doing more and sooner? Did he know that she sought refuge in the months and weeks before with another man? In spite of myself, I felt a growing kinship with him. I had been unreasonably angry with Ryan for a long time after his death. A divorce, even a painful one (and aren't they all painful?) is still preferable to death. In death there is such finality. All possibilities are lost. All chance for a last word, for reconciliation, for retribution dies with the other. How much harder must it be to look back, not at a fulfilling marriage, but instead at an unravelling tangle of lies and misery? I was Liz's friend, but like Michael, I was one of the survivors. We form a club whose membership is both burden and bond.

This was my thought as I entered the hotel lobby from the beach. I was shivering and wet, but I felt washed clean and peaceful, like when I woke from a dream in which I'd been crying. I walked to the elevator and pushed the button. I think I might have even been smiling.

The doors opened and I stepped back to let a man out. Instead, the man stopped directly in front of me.

I looked up in surprise into the face of Michael Bryson.

Chapter 5

HE SMILED WANLY.

"I just came from your room. You weren't there."

"I was taking a walk. On the beach." I was a little flustered, thinking about Bernie's confession, and even though it wasn't my infidelity, I felt an unaccountable shame.

"So I see." He inclined his head at my damp clothes and sandy feet.

There was an uncomfortable pause as we both stood facing each other. Perhaps because we were, in fact, a man and a woman, both alone, the territory felt new and unfamiliar to us. All I know is that it was really the first time I had been aware of Michael's hazel eyes, or the squareness of his chin.

I came back to myself with a nearly perceptible start.

"I'm sorry. Did you need something?" I asked.

"I know you probably think it's strange—my coming here. But I wanted to talk to you. This morning I... I just couldn't think straight. After you left, I had all of these questions." He ran his hand through his hair, looking frustrated at the awkwardness of language.

"I understand," I said, and I did. It was the first stage that followed unexpected death, the endless regurgitation of the last words, the last look, what they were thinking, what you wish you knew.

"Could we go somewhere to talk?"

I was shivering even in the warmth of the lobby. I told myself that that was why I said what I did.

"I need to get on some dry clothes. Do you want to come up while I change? We could order some coffee and talk there."

Michael nodded quickly, grateful to have this decision taken from him.

We rode the elevator silently, squeezed to one side by a heavyset, middle-aged woman with a dog cage who had entered just as the door closed. Once inside the room, I grabbed a fresh pair of jeans and a sweater from my bag and went in the bathroom to change. Michael called room service and ordered coffee. When I came out, he was standing by the sliding glass door, staring at the sea.

"I wonder stupid things... like is she cold... or was she scared," he said softly.

My first impulse was to go to him. I thought better of it, and sat on the edge of the bed instead.

"What did you want to talk about?"

He did not turn, but I saw his reflection in the glass. He had a twisted mouth, like a child trying not to cry.

"Liz. What else?" He dropped into the chair by the door, eyes still focused on the ocean. "Tell me, when Ryan died... did you hate him?"

"Sometimes. Yes. For leaving me. It was a broken promise."

He nodded to himself. "A broken promise. Do you know what I think, Sandi? I think she did it on purpose. One last grand dramatic gesture for everyone to see."

"Why do you say that?"

Michael turned just enough so he could face me. His eyes were hard and bitter.

"You knew her. It's something she would do."

I wanted to defend her, but I had known her, and it was just the sort of drama she would have appreciated. I changed the subject.

"How did you know where to find me?"

"Bill. The deputy. He checked around for me. I told him I wanted to thank you for coming into town on your white horse."

Anger was there.

"That wasn't my—"

"Yes, it was. She called you last night with some sob story and you came rushing in here to—to do what? Protect her from her evil husband? What is it you said this morning? To keep her out of an institution? Guess you were a few hours too late."

I flinched at the venom in his tone.

"I guess I was. But *she* called *me*, Michael. She asked me to come, so that's what I did. It wasn't a judgement on you."

34

"And what is it now?" he asked bitterly. "I have dead wife at the bottom of the Atlantic, and you must think I put her there. Oh, no, not directly—just by being married to her, isn't that it?"

I must have looked stricken.

"Jesus." Michael shook his head in disgust. "This is great, isn't it? I can't even believe it's me talking anymore. I'm sorry, I know you were just trying to help. This was a mistake. I'd better go."

He pushed back the chair abruptly and started for the door. Instinctively I stood in front of him, our bodies inches apart. He stopped short.

"It's okay," I said.

"It's not okay," he said, and grabbing both of my shoulders, pulled me to him roughly and kissed me.

His lips were hot and urgent, and his thumbs squeezed into the skin of my shoulders. It was more of an assault than an embrace, and he released me almost at once. He took a step back, breathing heavily as if he had been running, his eyes locked on mine.

"Let me go," he whispered.

I moved aside, and Michael Bryson brushed past me, opened the door, and left me standing alone.

Chapter 6

I WAS A HOT MESS OF indignation and shame and—if we are being honest—desire.

Of course, I rationalized what had happened. His anger, the same feeling of insane urgency that I could identify because I had seen it in myself, propelling me in the days after Ryan died. When I think of widows, I always picture Jacqueline Kennedy in that stained pink suit, head high, doing grief as if it was an advanced version of a debutante's ball. For me, it was not like that. I had been pulled kicking and screaming into widowhood, as if the sheer force of my emotions could have altered my reality. How much more would there have been if my marriage had been flawed in the way his seemed to have been? Or if I had been left with three babies? You could forgive someone a kiss under those circumstances.

I just hadn't found a way to rationalize my own reaction.

I should have sat up all night, replaying what happened, analyzing what he had done, what I had done, why I had not been the one to pull away. But the emotional extremes of the day had left me drained and empty, so instead I silenced my cell phone, lay down on the bed, closed my eyes, and slept for twelve straight hours. I do not even think I dreamed.

A bright early afternoon sun was flooding through the glass when I finally woke. I rolled over to peer at the time on my phone and saw that I had three missed calls and three voice messages.

The first was from Bernie Wathen.

"Hi, Sandi, it's Bernie from up at the high school... I, uh, thought you might be headin' back home today, and I just wanted to say thanks for the drink and all... and have a safe trip. Bye."

The second message was from Michael.

"Hi, Sandi. It's Michael. I'm sorry about last night. I don't know what happened... I know it's no excuse, but it's just been tough, you know? Anyway, I hate to ask you after I was such an ass, but you said to call you if I needed anything, and—look, I understand if you can't, but... I have to meet with the funeral home director about the memorial service at one-thirty, and I need somebody to watch the kids. It will only be about an hour. Their regular sitter's son has strep throat, and I really... Liz took care of these kinds of things, and I don't know that many people to ask...so..." A pause, then Michael's voice again, clear and direct. "Look, even if you can't, I'd still like to talk to you. Call me if you can. I'm at home. 301-555-6768. Thanks."

I felt a kind of tightness in my chest. I was not at all sure that seeing Michael Bryson was a good idea for either of us. I listened to the next message, but it wasn't him; it was nothing more than a minute of what sounded like city traffic followed by a hang-up—someone's mistake.

I looked down at the call log. I could call and say I was leaving, that I couldn't help him. He had probably found someone else by now anyway. Calling back was the polite thing to do.

A woman answered.

"Hello?"

"Hi. I'm trying to reach Michael Bryson. Is he available?"

The woman's voice sounded a bit possessive. "He's really busy right now. Who is this?"

"Sandi Beck. I'm returning his call."

A male voice in the background cut off her response, and then Michael was on the phone. I thought I heard relief in his voice.

"Sandi? Thanks for calling me back."

"I'm sorry it's so late. I overslept, I guess."

"That's okay. I don't need a sitter any more. One of my neighbors is going to watch the kids."

"Oh, all right, then." I struggled to think of something else to say.

"If you have time, I could still use your help. I'm supposed to—no, Terry, it's in there—" A pause while I heard a child whining, the neighbor's voice, and a commotion of dishes. "Sorry, Sandi. It's the whole thing with the funeral. I don't know what to do. I mean, I've never done anything like this before. Could you, I mean would you be willing to meet me over at the funeral home and help me make the arrangements for Liz? It's a lot to ask, I know, but you are the only person I know who…"

He stopped, hesitant to say the words, but I understood. Ryan's death gave me a pass into a world normally inhabited by the old and infirm, and my expertise with death was what Michael needed. I didn't feel like I could say no.

"Sure. What is the name of the funeral home?"

I could almost hear his relief. "It's Markham's on Main Street. The biggest house in town. You can't miss it." The whining in the background turned to a wail. "I've got to go. I'll see you at one-thirty. Thanks, Sandi."

As I dressed, I realized that everything I had seen of Michael Bryson seemed at odds with what I had thought I knew about Liz's husband. Not long after they had married, Liz had begun to complain about Michael. We both taught an evening class, and afterward we would often go over to Solomons, a touristy little town on the Patuxent River, and have dinner and a glass of wine. She was pregnant, and she felt that Michael had become a total stranger since their marriage. At the time, I had thought to myself that she had barely known him before they married, but it wasn't something I said. I just listened and offered sympathy because I knew it was what she wanted.

She had painted Michael as stodgy, boring, and emotionless. According to Liz, he showed no interest in sex upon finding out she was going to have a baby. He never wanted to go out or invite people over, preferring to sit in his office and read or work. He criticized her for what he called "extravagant spending" because she had her hair and nails done and because she liked expensive shoes. She even suggested that perhaps he was gay and had not come to terms with his identity.

"If it is that bad, why don't you leave him?" I finally asked after perhaps a dozen of these laments. We were sitting across from each other, and I was watching as her red manicured nails dug into the wooden table as she talked.

Liz looked at me as if I were someone she never met.

"Leave him? Now?"

"If you're that unhappy. Lots of women are single mothers."

"Leave him so I can work my ass off and come home to a screaming kid every night? I don't think so."

"You could give him custody," I said.

She shook her head. "Divorce wouldn't change anything. Once you have children, you're stuck with each other. My parents were divorced, but they still had to deal with each other because of us. No—I'm stuck, married to somebody forty going on sixty. "

I thought of Michael as I'd seen him with his children and as I'd seen him last night. I believed him to be kind and caring, but I had also seen the fire. Michael Bryson was a passionate man.

Perhaps she was right, and he had not understood her. But I knew now she had not understood him either.

And I thought I did.

Chapter 7

THE MARKHAM FUNERAL HOME IS a cavernous and imposing white Victorian house looming over the north end of Pineyfield's only real street. One might at first take it for a residence, but the circular driveway seems oddly out of place, as do the many chairs—not rockers—which line the spacious front porch. I noticed a service road to one side, marked with a small sign for further parking in the rear. I pulled in next to Michael's faded brown Ford Escort, which I recognized from his driveway, laden with car seats. A cement walk led to a side porch entrance.

Inside, the Markhams had furnished with what would pass here for elegance. Reproduction Louis XVI chairs lined the large hallway, flanking a large, marble-topped sideboard and tall gilt mirror. The walls were covered in a small, dark print paper, and the carpet was inches thick and plush enough to dampen any sound. Thus I was startled when a hand touched my elbow.

"May I help you?" The owner of the hand, a wizened little man with a fringe of white hair, peered up at me from behind thick glasses.

"I'm looking for Michael Bryson. He asked me to meet him here."

The man nodded and motioned to a heavy oak doorway at one end of the hall.

"He's already in the office with my brother. That way. May I get you something? Perhaps a cup of coffee?"

I assured him I was fine and started for the oak door. My heels sank into the heavy carpet and my ankle twisted, but I recovered quickly and knocked on the door. A few minutes passed and the door was opened by a replica of the little man who had greeted me.

"Miss Beck, I presume? Please come in. Mr. Bryson is expecting you."

Michael rose and stood behind the gentleman I took for one of the brothers Markham. He smiled faintly. He was pale, his face glistened with a thin sheen of sweat, as if he were feverish. He looked ill. Perhaps it was because it was a funeral home—embraces just seem to come naturally there—but I walked over and hugged him lightly, as a friend or sister might. Our eyes met for a moment, and I saw both relief and gratitude there.

"We were just going over the arrangements," Mr. Markham said smoothly, sliding behind his desk. We sat down.

"I was telling Mr. Bryson that in cases like this, sometimes the family likes to have a closed casket."

No salesman compares to a funeral home director. No other businessman must convince you to spend so much money on something you don't need for someone who will neither know nor care. I am not saying there is no afterlife. I am just saying that anyone there will not give a damn about a velvet-lined oak casket.

"Mr. Markham, there was no body," I said as delicately as I could. "The casket would be empty."

"Indeed, yes. The casket becomes a symbol of the loved one, an object on which the family can then focus their grief and mourn their loss. Many families have found the casket to have a healing quality in situations of this nature," Mr. Markham said, leaning forward over hands folded as if in prayer.

I thought of the house I had seen. Michael Bryson did not have the luxury of this type of grief.

Michael sat frozen beside me. I folded my own hands on the desk and leaned toward the old gentleman, mimicking his empathetic gaze.

"Mr. Markham, Mr. Bryson has three small children. I'm sure his wife would have rather seen her insurance money spent on trust funds for college than a casket she won't be using," I said, softly but firmly enough that he would not confuse it with weakness. "I am certain that a display of pictures of Liz with her family would do as much or more as a symbol for grief. Wouldn't you agree?"

The little man's only show of emotion was a rapid blink as he struggled to reassess the situation and any possible opportunities this presented.

"Why, yes, that is a lovely idea. Very fitting."

"Michael?" I asked, turning to him.

"Yes... that sounds right," he said automatically.

Mr. Markham dove into this new plan with forced enthusiasm. "Lovely, just lovely. You will need framing and an easel for display. Would you like us to—"

"Michael, do you want me to put together a photo collage, or do you want to do it?" I asked him, deftly taking the decision from Markham Inc.

"I can do that. It might be... it actually might help with Lizzie," he responded in a shaky voice.

"You will be wanting a web page designed, then, I'm sure. Something that family and friends can visit again and again, to keep her memory fresh. We offer plans for up to ten years, with annual updates. Let me show you some examples," Mr. Markham urged, retrieving a large embossed binder from his desk drawer.

"You know, I would imagine Liz's students would be more than willing to put something like that together if you felt you wanted it. Why don't you talk to the principal of the school and see what he thinks?" I turned to the funeral director. "It always seems so much more meaningful if things like that are done by friends, don't you think?"

Mr. Markham looked at me with barely concealed irritation.

"Then I suppose that's all we can do for you. Let me just go over what we agreed upon before the arrival of Ms. Beck," he said, with pointed emphasis on my name. "There will be a prayer service tomorrow morning at eleven led by Father Warren in the blue room and a private funeral service tomorrow afternoon at the church. Correct?"

"Yes. Thank you." Michael sounded unsure.

Mr. Markham caught the hesitation and looked back at Michael hopefully.

"If you want anything else—"

"We will certainly call you. Thank you so much for your help." I smiled at the old man as I placed a hand under Michael's arm and propelled him from his chair.

Mr. Markham walked us to the side door, trailed by his brother. As we stepped out on the porch, one of them shut the door sharply behind us.

Michael stepped into the cold sunlight and shook his head as if to clear it.

"Are you all right?"

He closed his eyes a moment and breathed deeply. Then he looked away.

"It's not something I expected to have to do. I thought I could handle this, but I don't know. It's harder than I thought."

"I know. I'm sorry."

We stood there awkwardly in the parking lot.

"I really appreciate your coming—especially after last night."

"That's all right. Don't worry about it."

Michael looked out over the parking lot. "Are you going to stay for the service?"

"Yes, I think so."

"Good. I guess I'll see you then," he said, and he turned and began walking toward his car.

"See you," I answered, turning away. I made it to my door before I heard his footsteps behind me.

"Look, I just—I'd like to talk to you. I feel like I'm losing it here, and I don't know what to do."

The words came out in a rush, fresh with pain.

"Sure. Is there somewhere you want to go?"

"Not here. I can't handle having to see anybody I know."

He thought a minute.

"You're staying over at the beach. Why don't we go over there? There's a place we used to go to sometimes—it's open year round." I watched as he realized what he had said.

"I know. It hurts, and it seems like it won't stop. But it won't last forever."

He smiled wanly. "I hope so. Right now it doesn't seem like it can get any worse."

"It won't, it will get better. I promise," I said.

I believed it when I said it. I should have known not to make promises I could not keep.

Chapter 8

I FOLLOWED MICHAEL BACK ACROSS the bridge into Ocean City. He passed my hotel and pulled into a parking lot on 46th street. The islands in the lot were planted with live palm trees that were currently encased in plastic. The sign, wooden with a Jamaican flair, said "Secrets." I thought about Liz and Bernie, and the things I knew I would not say.

The place had that Robinson Crusoe/Disney feel, a themed décor consisting of plaster rocks, fishnet walkways, and pieces of wooden boats hung on the walls. We were seated in an empty plastic-curtained gazebo overlooking the bay, kept warm by a kerosene heater in the middle of the floor.

"Thank you again for going there with me," Michael said after the waitress had taken our order. "I guess you saved me about seven thousand dollars. God knows, it's not like I have a fortune lying around. I knew it was ridiculous... an empty casket... but I worry about Lizzie and how she'll see all this... what she'll remember."

I nodded. Ryan's death had been hard enough. Afterwards I had often felt bitter because we had no children, no remainder of Ryan to love. I had not considered how difficult it would be to share death with a child without scarring her.

"I know you probably think I'm... some sort of monster or something," Michael said suddenly, his eyes intently focused on a flock of gulls flitting around a narrow dock outside. "But you've got to understand, things hadn't been good for a long time. I guess... I... it had gotten so difficult that at first, when the sheriff's department called, I was..." He stopped, swallowed, as if his mouth refused to say the words in his mind. "...relieved."

I don't know what I had expected. It wasn't this.

Women, to a fault, will side with each other against a man. In all the times I had listened to Liz's litany of complaints about Michael, I had never thought to blame her for their problems. If my friend was unhappy, even if I knew she was at times high strung and unreasonable, then it was still his fault. To listen to Michael now, to sympathize even a little after she was dead, seemed more of a betrayal than a kiss.

I did not say anything, and he did not seem to notice. His eyes were still on the bay.

"I guess I always blamed her for lying. It's not that I wouldn't have married her, but..."

I suppose I made a sound of surprise. His eyes flicked to me and he raised his eyebrows.

"You didn't know, then? I always thought you did," he said, a hint of bitterness in his voice. "We slept together on our first date. It wasn't something I usually do, but Elizabeth wasn't like the women I usually dated. She was... I don't know... impulsive, daring. We went out a few more times, and then she told me she was pregnant. I wasn't too thrilled at first... I am a planner, you know, I don't like surprises. But I was turning forty, and I felt like if I didn't get married soon, maybe it wasn't going to happen."

Michael reflected a moment before going on.

"It was my fault, too. I didn't really know Elizabeth—I mean, I thought she was like, you know, like a one of those bright abstract paintings—all color and shape, but it was hard to tell exactly what she really was. I didn't understand her, but on the surface, she was... compelling, even magnetic. My life until then was ordered, exact, planned out. Marrying her was... at first it was exciting, because she was so unpredictable."

I could see that he was lost in the memory of her. We sat silently, both of us thinking. Outside a gull cried loudly, and Michael shook his head.

"At first I didn't get too involved in her doctor's appointments. She didn't seem to want me there. But then, maybe sixteen weeks in, she had such bad morning sickness that she started losing weight."

"I remember," I said.

"Her doctor ordered a sonogram, and I insisted on going. She was on the table, and I was watching the screen. The baby was fine, moving around, healthy. From what she had told me, it should have been about twenty-one weeks, but the technician said it appeared to be a developmentally normal sixteen week-old fetus. So then I knew—she couldn't have been pregnant before we got married."

"What did Liz say?" I asked, already making excuses for her in my own mind.

He smiled faintly, "She said it must have been a bad test—you know, the pregnancy test. But I couldn't help it... I thought she had lied purposely so I would marry her."

In spite of my friendship with Liz, I thought she might have, too.

"Anyway, we tried to make the best of it. Even if she lied, I thought, you know, she did it because she loved me, because she wanted to have my child. There are worse reasons for getting married. And when Lizzie came, well, Lizzie was great, you know, a really happy baby, and I loved her from the minute I saw her. So I thought... I thought it would all be okay."

"But then Liz got sick."

Michael nodded. "Afterwards Elizabeth had all of those problems. She was depressed, she gained weight, and then she started to lose her hair—" He broke off as the waitress brought our drinks.

I remembered this, mostly from her first few phone calls after the move. She made it sound like a joke, but I understood from Michael's face that it had been much more than that. He resumed when the waitress walked away.

"It was... difficult to want to be physically intimate. That sounds bad, I know. Like I shouldn't have cared what she looked like. But it wasn't just outward appearance. She was so moody that sometimes I felt like I had married four different women, and I never knew which one I was coming home to. I tried...we saw a counselor... and for a while things seemed better. Then Elizabeth found out she was pregnant again, and we played the same cycle over. Just when it looked like we were coming out of it all again, she found out she was pregnant with our third. I know," he added defensively, though I had not said a word, "that that was my fault, too. But everything was complicated. You couldn't just kiss, or touch. You had to have reasons and explanations, you had to discuss what you really wanted—I felt like making love to her was a test every time, and I could never prove myself worthy, you know? If she gave in, that was what it was—giving in. So after the last baby I stopped trying."

We both stared out of the window and pretended to drink our wine. I wanted to speak up in Liz's defense, but I could see the scene as it must have happened, and I found myself pitying this quiet man who had literally married a whirlwind.

"I guess we would have gone on that way. I wouldn't have asked for a divorce because of the kids. We argued, but mostly about money, never about what was really wrong. Then, maybe five or six months ago, things changed. Elizabeth was way up, lots of energy. She'd work late, then come home and want to talk until one, two o'clock in the morning. She lost a lot of weight, got a new haircut—she looked great, but she was almost frantic, you know? Like someone had increased the speed of life just for her. I thought maybe she was taking something, some drug—I even searched through her purse, but I never found anything. This went on for a couple of months, and then—crash—she came down. I came home from work and she was in the bathtub crying, with all of these razor blades lined up on the edge. I freaked. I mean, the kids were there. The baby was lying there screaming, and Lizzie was trying to get him out of the crib, and Joshua..." His voice trailed off, his eyes reliving that day. He shook his head.

"We went to see another counselor, and she recommended a psychiatrist. He put Liz on antidepressants, and they seemed to help. But then the other night she just started crying and wouldn't stop. It went on for hours... it was loud, and the kids were scared, and then they started crying. I didn't know what to do. I called the doctor who was treating her and he changed her meds. I told her then that if she didn't stop..." Michael seemed to collapse and covered his face with his hand.

"That you would need to have her institutionalized?" I finished gently.

"Yes. So, you see," he said quietly, meeting my eyes, "I really did kill her. I sent her off that bridge as much as if I were driving the car."

He really had no idea Liz had been having an affair. He was shouldering all of the guilt for her death. Which would be kinder, to let him believe that it had been all about the two of them, or to tell him that she had betrayed their marriage and killed herself for the love of another man?

I shook my head.

"No. I would have done the same thing. You didn't have a choice, Michael."

He looked at me closely.

"Do you think she would say that?"

"I think she would now," I lied.

He was still for a moment, then nodded.

"Thank you. I hope that's true, but I guess there's no way to know. I wonder... after Ryan died, did you think about heaven and hell and all that?"

"Yes," I answered, remembering how often the questions of immortality had played out in my head as I lay tossing and sleepless.

"If she killed herself, do you believe that... that damns her?"

I shook my head.

"If she took her own life, it wasn't a rational decision. I have to believe that God, if He exists, is merciful enough to understand mental illness."

Michael agreed. "That's what I think, too. But for Lizzie's sake I don't want to even admit the possibility. I don't want her to feel like her mother abandoned her."

"She has you. You are a wonderful father."

"I don't know. I wasn't much of a husband."

Once I would have agreed with him. Now I was not so sure.

"We all do the best we can," I said, reaching for his hand and pressing it. "I do know that Liz always said how great you were with the kids."

The corner of his mouth turned up in a sad smile, and he did not move his hand. We both watched the water.

"You all want another drink?" the waitress asked.

I pulled back my hand and picked up my glass, draining the last of the wine.

"No," Michael answered, dropping a bill on the table. "That's it."

The waitress pocketed the money and walked away, empty glasses in tow. Without a prop, my hand dangled, useless.

"I need to get home," he said.

He had already started to rise. I formulated a smile, tried it on, and looked up.

"Of course. If I can do anything—"

"Thanks. I appreciate it."

I rose, and we both walked to the parking lot. Unable to bear another awkward moment, I walked directly to my car, putting its metal body between us.

"Sandi... thank you. For listening."

Michael was standing by his own open car door, his eyes on my face.

"No problem, "I said. "Anytime."

I got in the driver's seat, carefully buckled my seat belt, and pretended to search for my Ipod in the glove box until he pulled away.

Chapter 9

I STOPPED AT THE FOOD Lion and bought a paperback spy novel and then went to the liquor store and got a bottle of wine. Whether or not I wanted to admit it, the day had taken an emotional toll on me. The funeral home, the things I could have told Michael and didn't, and the empathy I felt for him that made me vulnerable to some deeper, unnamed caring... I didn't want to think about any of it, at least not for tonight.

I hadn't eaten lunch, and it was now late afternoon. Dining choices for single people are limited: eat at a restaurant table, reading so as not to look so painfully alone, or pick up take-out and eat it in the car. Neither option seemed terribly appealing, but a to-go meal at least had the virtue of being cheaper and it didn't require small talk or a tip.

I stopped at a deli to order a steak and cheese sub. On the way in I noticed a women's clothing store in the same strip a few doors down. I had come with a small bag that contained one clean set of casual clothes that I was currently wearing and certainly nothing appropriate to brave the halls of the Markham's tomorrow. I needed to find a dress for the prayer service, and I didn't feel like spending hours doing it.

The store was called Mia's. A few brightly colored Hawaiian print dresses and a bikini were displayed in the window, but a look inside showed a clearance rack of darker clothing. A ceiling light was on in the center of the shop, but otherwise it was deserted. A buzzer sounded as I entered, but no one appeared. I checked my watch—four o'clock. Perhaps they weren't really open after all.

"Hello?" I called out.

A teenaged girl emerged from a back room, IPad in hand, wearing shockingly black lipstick and an aggrieved expression.

"Can I help you?" she asked, though clearly she was hoping that she could not.

I explained that I was looking for a dark dress, navy or black, and preferably plain. She cast a longing look at the IPad and put it on the counter, then set off to the clearance end of the store.

"Over here. There's one with a jacket and one without, sizes six through ten. Do you wanna' try 'em on?"

I glanced at the two choices, then looked at the tags. Definitely pricey, especially for sale prices in the off-season. As the girl watched with barely concealed impatience, I shuffled through the rack and pulled out an eight in the cheaper design. It was a plain black sheath with three-quarter sleeves and a scooped neck, and it was still eighty dollars. I sighed.

"This is fine," I said. "I don't think I need to try it on."

The girl's eyes widened and she temporarily forgot her IPad.

"You sure? You almost never seen anybody make up their minds so quick."

"It's for a funeral service," I answered by way of explanation, although I seldom spend more than a few minutes shopping for clothes anyway. I hate shopping malls and buy everything online except jeans. I thought the salesgirl would probably faint if I told her I never even saw most of my clothes until UPS dropped them off.

Meanwhile she was nodding sagely, as the very young so often do when confronted with death. She took the dress over to ring up, apparently deciding that the sale was enough to warrant the loss of her time.

"Funeral? For that teacher?" she asked.

"Yes," I said, somewhat dismayed that I would now have to weather the uncomfortable speculations that always accompanied the unexpectedly deceased.

"You know, it's funny. She came in here just last week. I'm sure it was her, 'cause her picture's been in the paper, but she was different, too. You know, thinner. She came in and bought three whole outfits, top to bottom, without even looking at the price tag. Now some people are saying she killed herself, but why would you do that when you just bought new clothes? Cash or credit?"

She tacked the last sentence on to her breathless account without a change of tone, so it took me a minute to realize that she had asked me a question. I opened my wallet and fished out a credit card. She smiled.

"See, and almost nobody pays with cash anymore. Almost a thousand dollars. If I was gonna kill myself, I'd at least charge it. Wouldn't you?"

"I'm sorry?" I asked, feeling confused at the rapid shifts in conversation.

"I'm sayin', she paid cash. It came to nine hundred and sixty dollars. I don't forget a sale like that! It just doesn't sound like suicide to me. I think it must have been something wrong with her car. You know, you see all the time on the Internet how those car makers don't test things and then they lie about it. Sign here."

I signed, struggling between irritation at the girl's cavalier discussion of Liz's death and curiosity. Curiosity won out.

"What kinds of things did she buy?" I asked.

"You know, that was kinda' funny, too," she said, carefully folding and re-folding the dress so that it would absolutely need to be ironed. "You can see we've got our spring and summer stock in, but it's been so cold, it hasn't moved. She bought all warm weather clothes, and real pale pastel colors. Now, I'm studying cosmetology, and she was a winter, you know? Dark hair, brown eyes. Or maybe a fall. And she was buying like a summer. I even said to her that, you know, she might look better in the reds. I mean, I said it nicely, 'cause she was spendin' all that money and I didn't want to piss her off." She glanced up at me quickly to see how I would take her language, and I smiled benignly. She nodded and went on, folding the top of the shopping bag and sliding it across the counter as she spoke.

"She just laughed and said she was ready for a change. Sad, isn't it? I guess she got one all right."

I thanked the girl and started to turn away. Then I caught a glimpse of her computer screen: bright yellow and black edges, a webpage layout I immediately recognized as Cliff notes.

She saw my interest.

"Did you ever read this? It's pretty cool."

She passed the tablet to me. *Les Miserables.*

"I read the novel," I answered.

"The whole novel? That's like five hundred pages. I just read these. It gives you the whole story, and you don't have to spend all that time. Kind of like *Soap Opera Digest.* Have you ever read that?"

I fled from the store before she could expound on the advantages of reading about bad television as opposed to watching it and headed back to my hotel. I hung up the dress in the bathroom in the forlorn hope that the humid air would steam out the teenager-induced wrinkles. I then eased into a hot bath, drank a glass of wine, and settled into that big chair that sat like a watchman by the sliding glass balcony door. I opened the novel and tried to lose myself in the world of espionage, but it was as if it were my sophomore chemistry book—my eyes swept from one side to the other again and again, but the words refused to lodge anywhere.

I dropped the book on the floor, turned off the light, and stared out into the night. It isn't Michael, I thought firmly, and I was surprised to find that this was true. He was there, of course, in the forefront of my mind, but he wasn't what was bothering me. Something was churning, just beneath the surface, and I could not put it into words. I had the sense of something, something, just beyond my grasp. I closed my eyes, and then I saw it.

Bernie Wathen's broad forearm lying across the Formica tabletop. It had borne the familiar eagle wings of a Harley Davidson.

A motorcycle.

The deputy had said that the only other vehicle near the scene was a motorcycle. Its rider had not slowed or stopped for the frightened man who had just watched Liz's car plunge from the bridge into the cold water. I had wondered then, why would Liz have gone to a dead end road leading into a closed park just before sunset? The idea that she had planned her death seemed at odds with that phone call an hour before, pleading for my help. Why would she call me, get my promise to meet her the next day, and then drive straight to a secluded park, wait at least a half hour, and then drive off a bridge? Factor in the shopping trip the week before, and it didn't make sense.

Unless she had not been alone for that half-hour. Unless she had gone to that dead end road to meet someone who couldn't—or shouldn't—be seen with her.

I let it run, then, without restraint. I imagined her, perhaps planning to run off with Bernie. Shopping, getting new clothes for a clandestine trip to some island. Then I imagined him telling her that he couldn't go, things were too touchy at home. People might find out. She would have been hurt, angry. I imagined her sitting at her desk, talking to me, and perhaps Bernie coming in. I played it in my mind like a movie I was directing. The door might have been locked. He would have seen she was on the phone, crying. He would have gotten out his key, opened it... I remembered the sound of a door, and a man's voice. She would have hung up quickly, maybe tried to push past him. He would have grabbed her arm, asked her to meet him. *We have to talk, but not here... I know of a place*—and she would have driven to that road, that park, and he would have followed her.

So how had it gone from there? Had he told her it was really over, and had that caused her to take her life? *I can't see you anymore. I know you'll understand...* I tried to picture her sobbing, hysterical, jamming the gas pedal to the floor and squealing tires, tears flowing down her face. But this didn't feel real, even as a film in my head. It seemed a long leap from calling him an asshole to purposely ending her life for want of him. Having talked with Bernie Wathen across a beer, I could see a lonely woman having an affair with him, but...

A sudden, piercing idea stabbed me. I sat paralyzed, unwilling to think it but unable to dismiss it.

Suppose it had gone another way? Suppose Liz had gotten angry and threatened to expose Bernie, to go to his wife? She might have even done it, and he was the sort of man who counted his worth by his golf partners, his softball batting average, and his membership in the Elk's Lodge as much as by the notches in his belt for lonely young teachers. His standing, his face in the community, was the only real wealth for an underpaid public servant in a small town.

Could Bernie Wathen have killed Liz Bryson and tried to make it look like an accident?

I played the scene again. This time I imagined him sliding into the passenger seat beside her. The air would have been cold. I could imagine her leaving the car running for warmth, and perhaps to make a point. *You have five minutes and I'm leaving...* and the sweat starting on his forehead. *Who were you talking to? You know we have to be careful, my wife is getting suspicious.*

I could imagine her laugh, high and edgy, I could hear her voice, the scornful note. *I guess you should have thought about that before now, Bernie. Why should I be the only one to pay?* Perhaps he hit her then, knocked her unconscious, and in his fear he—he what? He drove her car to just below the crest of the bridge, wedged her foot onto the pedal, put it in gear, and watched her fly off and down, down... and as soon as he heard the splash he walked back to his bike and took off. Then there would have been a moment of terror, blowing by the retired fisherman waving his arms, the fisherman who might be a witness.

I stood and began to pace. This was insane. Liz had been unstable according to both her husband and her lover. Why did I insist on directing this B movie to come up with some logical excuse for her death? Is there ever a suicide that is logical and reasonable?

And yet, if Bernie had done it, if he had taken her life, who in Pineyfield would come forward to accuse him? The deputy was his brother. Michael was exhausted and struggling between guilt and relief. No one seemed inclined to even ask questions. It would be better for everyone to bury the memories in lieu of her body and forget it all, let it slip past like the current, move on. The role of avenging angel could fall to me... and that in itself was laughable. I knew no one here. I had not been her best friend in life, and I was likely not her truest mourner in death.

At this point I decided that my whole line of thought was the product of a difficult day and an overactive imagination. I turned off the light and went to bed, determined to put the whole thing from my mind.

But when I dreamed, I dreamed of murder.

Chapter 10

THE NEXT DAY DAWNED BRIGHT and clear. I opened the glass door to the balcony and drank in the chilled salt air. The warmth of the morning sun gave the slightest hint of coming spring. Standing there, looking out at the gently rolling waves, my theories from the previous night seemed melodramatic at best. Accidents happen. People die. There is not always a motive or even a reason, and to set off blindly in search of one is ultimately disappointing. If I hadn't learned that yet, after years of trying to construct meaning from Ryan's death, I was a fool.

I glanced at the clock on the night table and saw that it was nearly ten. Sleeping in seemed to be all I had done since arriving here. I showered and changed into the dress, which looked only slightly bedraggled. Then I set off for the funeral home, stomach already growling and no time to eat on the way.

Cars lined the Pineyfield streets leading to the funeral home. A somber, middle-aged man who bore a striking resemblance to the two Markham brothers stopped my car at the entrance.

"Family of the deceased?"

"No, a friend."

"The lot is full, miss. You'll need to find a space back on the street," he said, waving to the area behind me.

I backed out and turned, finally spotting an empty space along the curb at least a half a mile away. Fortunately I was wearing the same black flats I wore with jeans, so the hike in the open air was almost therapeutic. As I approached the funeral home, I saw that the porch was packed with teenagers and their parents, many crying. I squeezed past them and inside, where throngs of people stood in the wide hallway talking in hushed voices. On the right, at the entrance to a small side room, a brass stand held a card with the name Bryson neatly printed in gold on deep blue paper. I couldn't help wondering if the gold embossing cost extra. Shaking my head slightly at my own cynicism, I joined what seemed to be a line of people and followed them slowly inside.

The room was thickly carpeted in royal blue, with blue and gold raised wallpaper in a pattern that resembled crowns. A few rows of upholstered straight-backed chairs, mostly empty, faced forward, where Michael stood in an open area at the front of the room. People were filing past him one at a time, shaking his hand and offering whispered condolences. A few teenagers clung to each other in the back corner, sobbing against a backdrop of softly muted organ music. Two large picture frames had been placed on easels along the sides of the room. I slid from the line and walked over to one. It was a collage of snapshots of Liz, everything from what must have been a few of her own faded baby pictures to her wedding photograph with Michael. I guessed that the frame on the other side contained family pictures from the past few years.

Another woman came to stand beside me. She was small, bony, and birdlike, with pale bleached hair that seemed varnished into place. Her face was unpleasantly sharp, her eyes small, and I confess that I took an instant dislike to her based solely on appearance. She must have noticed my gaze, for she looked up and smiled thinly.

"Friend of the family?"

I nodded.

"Didn't think I'd seen you around here. Were you close to her?" she asked, nodding at the photographs.

Something about her tone, some edge of aggression, warned me off.

"No, not really. We hadn't seen each other in years," I said politely, which wasn't really a lie.

"She was disturbed, you know," the woman confided with something akin to pleasure in her eyes.

"No, I... I wasn't aware of that," I answered, struggling to keep my voice level.

"Bernie told me. My husband," she added. "She worked for him over at the high school. He did what he could for her, but..." She shrugged as if to indicate that some things can't be fixed.

I nearly laughed aloud. So this was Mrs. Wathen.

"Her death must have been hard for him," I said, praying that my face was not transparent.

She peered at me closely, as if suspecting I was being sarcastic. She must have decided I was sincere, because she sighed somewhat dramatically.

"It was, yes, it was, but I can't say it was really a surprise. You know, I was the one who had to tell him." Leaning closer, she added, "He was late getting home—he puts in so many hours, you know—and when his brother called I thought at first, Lord, something has happened to Bernie. It's that motorbike, you know. I can't understand why a grown man would want to ride around on that thing. But then he told me—Bernie's brother, I mean—they thought it was that woman, she was missing, and they had some report that a car had gone and driven right off the Assateague Bridge. Bernie got home right after that, and he looked so tuckered out that I thought, bad news can wait. I let him go on and shower, and then let him eat his dinner. You don't want to deal with shock on an empty stomach. And then I told him."

"That must have been awful," I said, struggling to infuse my voice with warm sympathy.

Mrs. Wathen nodded, enjoying her role. "It was, believe me. But, like I said, not a surprise. She had been so unbalanced. She had been," her voice dropped to a whisper, "hospitalized, you know. For a mental thing."

"I heard something along that line," I answered.

"Well, what will be, will be," Mrs. Wathen said stoically.

Before I could answer, I felt movement behind me, and found myself looking up into Bernie Wathen's red, perspiring face.

"This is my husband now. —Bernard Wathen, meet Miss…I'm sorry, I didn't catch your name."

"No, you didn't," I said smoothly. "Please excuse me."

I turned and walked away, leaving Mrs. Wathen looking after me, puzzled, and Mr. Wathen mopping his brow with a handkerchief. I turned the corner and stood out in the hallway, away from the flow of traffic. A heavyset woman in an impossibly purple dress wandered up and stood beside me.

"You must be Liz's friend from out of town," she said in a companionable voice.

"Is it that obvious?" I asked.

She chuckled deeply. "Sweetie, you sure don't look like you're from around here. Besides, I either grew up with, diapered, or am kin to nearly every soul here except for Michael Bryson, so I suppose I do have an advantage. I'm Betty Ann Oriwitz. I'm one of the secretaries over at the high school. I heard all about you from Sally Morgan's girl, who lives next door to the Brysons."

"I see," I said a trifle coolly.

"Now don't get your back up, dear. That Lilly Morgan's hot to trot, always has been. I take anything she says with a grain of salt. As for that, anybody who is a friend of Liz's is a friend of mine. I really liked that girl. Just between you and me and the lamp post, anybody who tells me that girl killed herself is barkin' up the wrong tree."

"Why do you say that?"

"People who take their own lives—and I'm speaking from experience here, my brother Mike hung himself in the garage eighteen years ago this July—well, those people are quiet-like. They make up their minds to go, and they are at peace, seems to me. Now she was still spittin' mad when she left work."

"You talked to her before she left?"

"Oh, not exactly. You see, I'm Mr. Wathen's secretary. They must have been havin' an argument elsewhere, and he storms in, and she storms in right after him. He shut the door." Betty Ann grinned. "But those walls are paper thin. She's yellin' and he's just tryin' to calm her down, like. Finally it gets quiet, and then she leaves. The next thing you know, he leaves. Makes you wonder now, doesn't it?"

"Do you think they were going to meet somewhere?"

This was too direct for Betty Ann. She shrugged.

"Not for me to say."

"Miss Oriwitz, have you gone to the police with this information?"

"The police?" She looked at me like I'd grown a second head. "You must have misunderstood me, darlin'. Around Pineyfield, we don't tell tales on our neighbors."

She moved away from me quickly, as if she feared I was catching. I stood against the wall, weighing everything I had heard.

Liz and Bernie argued.

They left work at about the same time.

But Bernie had not gone right home, and according to Mrs. Wathen, his brother's call had come much earlier than seven-thirty. Why had he lied to me? Where had he been during that missing hour? It seemed an unlikely coincidence that his whereabouts for the time of Liz's death were unknown, and that a motorcycle was seen crossing the bridge just minutes after her car plunged into the water. Could it have been Bernie's?

This wasn't just late night imagination. This was evidence. Wathen had motive and opportunity. I was starting to believe that adultery was the least of Bernie Wathen's sins.

Chapter 11

I HAD FULLY INTENDED TO stay for the service, but suddenly I felt compelled to leave, to literally shake the dust of Pineyfield from my shoes and to seek the peace of my boat. I made my way to Michael to offer my condolences and say goodbye. He stood in a small alcove, a line of people waiting to speak to him. He seemed glazed over, as if only a facsimile of Michael Bryson stood there, a shell really, shaking hand after hand and listening to the polite regrets of faceless strangers, as well as weathering the loud and sometimes sloppy protestations of sorrow from scores of melodramatic teenagers.

Witnessing this was like pulling an adhesive patch from a scabbed wound. My memory of the days after Ryan's death were open, and they burned. Add to that the swirling accusations and doubts that were playing in a closed loop in my brain, and I realized I had nothing of value to offer him. I don't think he even noticed when I slipped away.

I went back to the hotel and packed, then checked out without even a backward glance at the ocean that could so lure me. I wasn't taking any chances. I climbed in my car and headed for the road home.

I have said before that guilt is a powerful thing. I already felt the vague and definite stirrings of the need to do something, and the doomed sense that if I did not, then it would be my fault that nothing was ever done. The intensity of these feelings increased as I neared, and then passed, the turn south toward Virginia. Disgusted with myself, I did a U-turn and found my car, as if of its own volition, directly in front of Pineyfield's police station.

Bill Wathen looked up at me in undisguised surprise and swung his feet off his desk.

"Miz Beck, this is a surprise. I thought you'd be over at the service."

"I was. I need to talk to you."

He digested this for a moment in his slow, thoughtful way. He did not look happy.

"I would've thought we didn't have much else to talk about."

"I thought so, too. But now I really feel there are some things we need to clear up," I said, trying to keep my voice from displaying my nervousness.

"Clear up," he repeated, clearly unconvinced.

I sat down opposite him, which didn't do much to improve his mood.

"Deputy, I think there are certain facts about Elizabeth Bryson's death that could use further investigation."

"Do you, now," Bill Wathen said in a thin voice.

"I do. I know this is awkward for you, but I—well, I just don't think this is a time when it is appropriate to look the other way."

"I thought we had agreed it was in the best interest of those children to rule the death an accident," the deputy said slowly.

"That was when I thought it was a suicide, Deputy—not a murder."

There was a sharp hissing intake of breath.

"You might want to think a minute before you say much more," Bill Wathen said quietly. "Accusing someone of murder is a serious charge. You might find yourself on the wrong side of a jail cell door."

"Are you threatening me, Deputy?" I asked, feeling a cold knot growing in my stomach.

"No ma'am, I am just stating the obvious."

"Then let me state the obvious for you, Officer," I said, angry now. "Did you do any forensic tests on Elizabeth Bryson's car when you pulled it from the river? Did you question anyone at the high school about her past relationships, or who might have had a motive to kill her? Did you ask your brother where he was when she was killed, when you found out he wasn't home when you called from the park that evening? Did you—"

He rose, his face purple with rage.

"Get out! Get out now!"

"You can cover for him all you want, Deputy Wathen, but I'm just saying what half the people in that school probably already think. How long are you going to be able to keep a lid on that?"

I turned my back to him and pushed out the door. I heard a noise like a fist hitting a file cabinet, but I did not look back. In the hallway outside, two young men in uniforms moved away quickly, their eyes focused on the floor as I passed. There was no doubt that every word we said would be circulated at Pineyfield's dining room tables that night. But it wouldn't be enough.

I drove home almost without thinking. When I turned into the road to the marina some six hours later, I couldn't recall a single mile I had driven or landmark I had seen. I pulled into the parking lot in the fading late afternoon light, opened the car door, and breathed in the stillness.

My boat is nestled in a slip on Carter's Creek in Irvington, a tiny one-street tourist town. The summer sees the big resort hotel and the bed-and-breakfast fill and the anchorage pack with pleasure boats, but on March afternoons like this one, the marina was deserted. Except for the rustling of a squirrel in the pine trees across the street and the occasional harsh bark of a heron, it was absolutely silent.

I walked down the weathered dock to my sailboat, loosened the lines, and climbed aboard. The cabin was damp—I turned off the heater when I left—so I started the little ventless propane fireplace and crawled into the V-berth. It felt hollow, cold, and clammy, and it was the only home I had. I closed my eyes and slept.

I woke perhaps an hour later, but already the cabin was the gray of twilight. The sun was low in the sky, a few rays filtering through the tinted portholes. I knew I had made a decision in my sleep, and I acted on it. I fished my cell phone from my purse and called Wayne Kremm.

I had met Wayne years ago when he had done a guest lecture at the college. We had invited him out on our boat, and he and Ryan became friends. Later, after Ryan's death, he called to check on me weekly, even when I wouldn't answer the phone. He was the one who had recommended me for the writing job. In the last two years we had struck up a tentative friendship of our own based on mutual interests and his rather misguided hope that he could sleep with me. Nothing had come of it, but we remained on friendly terms. None of which was why I called him.

Wayne Kremm was an investigative reporter for the *Washington Post*.

"Hey, what's hangin'?" he answered his phone in his characteristically cheerful voice.

"Wayne, it's Sandi Beck."

His voice grew warmer.

"Sandi! Babe, I knew you'd come around someday! My place or yours?"

"Neither. Listen, Wayne, I think I have a story for you."

"Really? Local ex-English prof poses for Playboy?"

Wayne had never developed an understanding of political correctness. It was what I liked best about him.

"Close. I've got an English teacher in a small eastern shore town who drove her car off a bridge—only I don't think she was actually driving. About half the town knows she's been sleeping with the main suspect, who would be her boss at the local high school, who just happens to be the deputy sheriff's brother. They had an argument just before, and some evidence suggests he was there when it happened. No body, no investigation. Interested?"

I had tried to put a little *Dateline* in my voice. Wayne took it eagerly.

"How recent?"

"Her funeral service was this morning."

I could hear him thinking.

"Tell me this is close to a certain popular tourist location, and I will definitely be interested."

"Pineyfield, right outside of Ocean City. And, Wayne—the car went off the bridge in a national park."

"I knew I loved you. F.B.I. called in yet or are the U.S. Park Police handling it?"

"Neither as far as I know. Just the local sheriff's department."

He made a contented sound.

"Sounds like the perfect formula for a cover-up. Name of the dearly departed?"

"Elizabeth Bryson."

"You're a doll. Hey, Sandi, what's in this for you?"

I paused.

"She was a friend."

He adjusted his voice accordingly.

"Geez, I'm sorry. I'll, uh... I'll get on it. Justice and all that."

"Thanks, Wayne."

"Not a problem. If you want to get together and talk, maybe—"

I smiled.

"No. But thanks."

"Thank you."

He hung up, and I knew as soon as he did he would be tracking the story down. Wayne was good at his job, and he did it without scruples. That is exactly what Pineyfield needed.

I made a cup of tea, took a shower, and crawled back into bed.

Chapter 12

A WEEK WENT BY, IN WHICH I resumed as much of my former life as possible. I finished off an article for *Northern Neck Style* and shipped it off, then spent two days arguing with a hierarchy of representatives from a gold distributor who had sold my eighty-year old client collectible coins at 600 percent over market value. It was only after I suggested I was an investigator for *AARP Magazine* that they agreed to refund her money—not exactly a lie, since my client was a member, and she did intend to write a letter to the editor.

After that the weather grew slightly warmer, and I spent three days sanding the teak rails on the topside of my boat and beginning the painstaking job of varnishing. At night I read, book after book, until I fell asleep with the pages open and the book propped against my chest. I pushed Michael from my thoughts, convinced myself I was removed from the situation, that it was over at least as far as I was concerned. Then, on Sunday, Michael called.

It had been a June-like morning but a cold front was forecast for the afternoon. I had just put on the final coat of varnish and was washing up when the phone rang.

"Who the hell do you think you are, Sandi?"

Michael Bryson.

"What are you talking about?"

He laughed bitterly.

"Don't insult my intelligence. I know you set him on to it. Who else would have done it? Did you even read what he wrote? Bill Wathen called. The F.B.I. is coming in. Is that what you wanted?"

My stomach lurched.

"Are you talking about Wayne Kremm? What did he write?"

He swore for a few minutes, and it seemed so out of character that it frightened me. He didn't answer me until he finished.

"Read the Sunday *Post*, Sandi. He wrote it all, every whisper, every piece of gossip in this town. It's all there—Liz's affair with Wathen, her breakdown, their fight—there's even a great picture of Lizzie on page three."

"Michael, I'm sorry," I took a deep breath. "I didn't mean for you to get dragged into this."

"What did you think would happen? She was my wife, for God's sake."

I felt like an idiot. I really hadn't expected this. What had I thought? That Liz's murder would be investigated totally apart from her beautiful children or her handsome, betrayed husband? They made such obviously good copy.

"I didn't think," I said honestly. "I just wanted justice, Michael. I wanted him to pay. I didn't think about you, or the children... I'm sorry."

There was silence. I waited.

When he spoke again, his voice was tired.

"I wish you had told me. It would have been better if I had been ready, that's all."

"I couldn't. I just... I didn't know how. It wasn't until the day of the funeral service that I really thought he was involved," I explained haltingly.

"Yeah. Well."

There was another long, painful pause.

"It's been a zoo around here. Reporters everywhere. We walk down the aisles in the grocery store and everyone stops and stares at us. I feel like I should wear a shirt, you know? Something that says 'Yes, I was her husband, and no, I didn't know.'"

"Maybe you should take some time off, take the children away for a few days," I suggested lamely.

"I am. I called my parents in Pennsylvania. We're leaving tonight and driving out there for two weeks. That's all the PTO I have. Maybe by then this will all blow over."

"Maybe," I said uncertainly.

There was another pause.

"Do you... do you really think he killed her?" Michael asked.

"Yes."

"I know it doesn't make much sense, but I hope you're right."

He hung up the phone then, without saying goodbye. And I understood what he meant. Murder, at least, is a reason.

Chapter 13

I FOLLOWED THE PAPERS RELIGIOUSLY for the next few weeks. Liz's story made the Maryland and Washington, D.C. papers first, and then the local nightly news, and it finally hit the networks when Bernie Wathen was arrested for second degree murder.

It started like Michael had said. The F.B.I. came in and did forensic tests on the car. Sure enough, they found fibers from Bernie Wathen's polyester pants, his fingerprints on the dash and the wheel, and the coup de grace, a single strand of hair caught in the Velcro of a sunglass holder that matched his own DNA perfectly. I thought of how that must have smarted, for a balding man to be charged based on a hair. And, of course, that wasn't all. They found spots of Liz's blood on the carpet of her car, and after they obtained a search warrant, they found traces of her blood on Bernie's leather jacket. It was all they needed. Two weeks after Liz's memorial service, Bernie was arrested and placed in federal custody.

The fallout didn't end there. Bill Wathen resigned as deputy sheriff, and an investigation into his misconduct was pending. Bernie's wife promptly filed for divorce. The Pineyfield school board, a day late to this party, put Bernie on administrative leave without pay pending the outcome of his trial.

So it should not have been a surprise when federal investigators came knocking at my hatch, so to speak.

There were two of them, both dressed in dark navy suits with white shirts and dark, colorless ties. I was lying on the foredeck, reading a book and soaking up the sun of an unusually warm April afternoon. I heard them as soon as they stepped on the dock. Dress shoes have a distinctive sound on bare, dry wood. I sat up as they approached the boat.

"Hi," I said, rising and going forward in the hope that I could cut them off before they boarded. Otherwise, it could take me hours to scrub off the dark sole marks on the white deck.

"Are you Ms. Sandra Beck?" asked the first man, distinguishable from the other only by a slightly lighter shade of dishwater hair and a pair of wire-rimmed glasses.

"That's me. What can I do for you?" I asked, extending a hand in what I hoped was a relaxed fashion.

Nothing makes a saint feel like a sinner quite so effectively as a federal investigator, and I was no saint.

The second man flipped open a badge rather than proffer a hand. "F.B.I., Ms. Beck. I'm Agent Crawly, and this is Agent Bauer. We are working in conjunction with the U.S. Park Police. We have a few questions."

I noticed the dockmaster and two of the guys from the yard standing in the parking lot, watching us. I had been something of a mystery to the marina staff since I moved here. I could only assume they were waiting to see if I would be arrested. I looked down at the agents' shoes, then back at the workers. Now the marina manager was coming out of his office, too.

"Do you want to come aboard?" I asked.

This seemed to puzzle the two men. They stood motionless, exchanging looks.

"We could go inside," I suggested, motioning to the cabin.

They seemed to understand this at least, and both men climbed awkwardly over the lifeline and on to the bow. If you have never watched an F.B.I. agent in dress clothes and black leather shoes board a sailboat at high tide, I can only tell you that it is a valuable comic experience. I pinched my leg to keep from smiling and again extended a hand, which was this time taken with some measure of gratitude.

Once inside the cabin, the one called Crawly took out a pad and paper. Bauer asked the questions.

"Ms. Beck, you were acquainted with Elizabeth Bryson, now deceased, of Pineyfield, Maryland?"

"Yes."

One word clearly constituted an unsatisfactory answer. Bauer scowled.

"How long had you known Ms. Bryson?"

"A few years. We taught together, I don't know, maybe five years ago. I hadn't seen her in at least the last three or four years."

"Yet she called you on the night of March ninth and asked you to come to help her?" Crawly interjected.

"Yes."

"Why would she call you, Ms. Beck?"

Something about his attitude irritated me. I guess a little rebel is in all of us.

"I don't know, Agent Crawly. You could ask her, but she's dead."

Bauer's face grew pink to the tips of his ears. Crawly interceded before he could speak.

"Now, we know this is difficult, Ms. Beck. But we are trying to establish a sequence of events for the night Ms. Bryson died. Could you help us out here?"

He gave me his best attempt at a charming smile, and I relented and recounted the story as I remembered it. Barr broke in just as I was finishing up with my decision to drive to Pineyfield.

"Several witnesses have suggested that you were the first one to suspect that Ms. Bryson's death was not an accident. What basis did you have for these suspicions, Ms. Beck?"

"Agent Bauer, I did not know Liz was dead until I got to her house. The next thing I know, I am being questioned by the police and then Mr. Wathen calls me at my hotel and asks to meet with me. He said he heard I had suspicions. Before that moment, I really didn't have any. Maybe in the back of my mind I thought he might have been involved with Liz, but that was only because she said his name. I had not even been in town one day. I certainly hadn't seen anything to indicate he had killed her."

They did not respond, so I continued. "I was not the first person to say she didn't kill herself. Pineyfield is a small town. Everyone knew something was wrong, but no one wanted to hurt anyone by saying so. I was just the first person willing to do something about it."

"Why?" It was Crawly this time, and he seemed genuinely interested.

"I guess I felt guilty, Agent Crawly. I mean, she called me."

"Ms. Beck, why do you think Ms. Bryson called you?" Bauer asked.

"I told you. She wanted my help."

Bauer's eyes drilled into me.

"What exactly do you think you could have done to help Ms. Bryson that couldn't have been done by someone else in Pineyfield?"

He sounded accusatory, as if my agreement to go to Liz had somehow led to her death.

"What do you mean?"

"If Ms. Bryson simply needed a friend to talk to, any of her co-workers would have been a more reasonable alternative than an old friend who lived hundreds of miles away."

He let that sink in, and Crawly took over.

"I understand that you work as a kind of legal advocate, isn't that right?"

"Something like that."

"Is it possible, Ms. Beck, that Ms. Bryson anticipated that something could go wrong and she wanted you there because of that expertise? Is it possible she wanted to take some kind of action against Mr. Wathen, perhaps for sexual harassment, but she was afraid to do so?" Crawly asked.

"If you're asking if I think she knew she was in some kind of physical danger, no, I don't think so," I said, though I had wondered this myself. "I went in a clothing store in Ocean City to get a dress for the funeral, and the salesgirl starting talking about Liz's death. She told me that Liz had just been in there a few days before buying a lot of expensive summer clothes. That sounds... I don't know, too optimistic for someone who feels like their lover might try to kill them."

Both men looked at me as if I were too naive for words. I suppose the word "optimistic" is not one they hear used very often. Crawly did pick up on the shopping.

"Summer clothes, you said? Beach clothes?"

"It sounded like it."

"A little cold for that in March. Do you remember the name of the store?"

At the moment I didn't, but I gave directions that should put them on the same block. Crawly seemed to be pursuing a mental line of thought.

"Did she mention any kind of trip, perhaps to the Caribbean, Mexico, or Bermuda?"

"No. But we only talked for a few minutes that night, and like I said, she was upset. You'd have to ask someone else."

Crawly nodded. He and Bauer exchanged looks.

"I think we're about finished, Ms. Beck. Thank you for your cooperation. I will tell you that you will be subpoenaed to appear at Mr. Wathen's trial. "

I nodded, but I felt sick. Another thing I hadn't considered.

"If we need anything else, we'll be in touch. Good afternoon."

The men left, and I sank down on the bunk, wondering exactly what kind of Pandora's Box I had opened.

Chapter 14

ANOTHER FEW WEEKS PASSED UNEVENTFULLY. It was early May now, alternating days of unending downpour—rain falling in sheets and torrents, its sound making a wild and melancholy music—with days of clean, fresh sunshine, so new that they squeaked. Today had been the latter, and I kayaked around the creek and walked through the town. Now the sun was hanging low in the sky and the air cooling. I put on a sweater and sat out in the cockpit, reluctant to lose any minute of the day. I had my laptop balanced on my knees, finishing up case files, when the phone rang.

"Sandi, do you have a T.V. on that tub of yours?"

It was Wayne Kremm, and he sounded excited. I overlooked the disparaging comment. Wayne loved the water almost as much as I did, but he was a power boater all the way. He didn't leave the dock without an ice-maker, blender, and a microwave. He thought that my sailboat, with its spare, narrow berths and minimal conveniences, was comparable to tent camping.

"Yes, Wayne. I even have my own hot spot and a computer," I answered facetiously. "Is there any particular reason for the question?"

"Turn it on. Now. Channel four."

I climbed down the steps and grabbed the remote. It was really redundant—I have a twenty-inch screen, so I still have to be within an arm's length to see it.

"So what's up?" I asked as I switched it on.

"Just watch."

I sat through the end of a short piece on liposuction.

"Wayne, are you trying to offend me or what?"

"No—not that one. It should be next. Here."

The anchor looked gravely at the camera, "Now we'd like to get back to that breaking news story we told you about at the top of the hour. Andrea?"

The picture shifted to a pretty young woman in a navy blazer who stood outdoors against the backdrop of a nondescript municipal building.

"Good evening, Lance. I am standing in front of Atlantic Hospital in Berlin, Maryland, where officials have just confirmed that Bernard Wathen died of a gunshot wound to the head in what police are calling a suicide. Wathen was out on bond awaiting trial in a federal court for the murder of Elizabeth Bryson which took allegedly took place on National Park Service property. Bryson's car drove off of a bridge and into the river in what the prosecution claimed was a staged suicide planned and executed by Wathen. Mrs. Bryson was a teacher in the school where Wathen was a vice principal, and evidence suggests the two were involved in an affair gone bad. Wathen's wife had recently filed for divorce following the highly publicized investigation and arrest of her husband for the murder of the woman police believe was his lover.

"Police are telling us that Wathen was found by a neighbor after a gunshot was heard coming from his residence shortly after two p.m. this afternoon. We reported on April eighteenth that Wathen's brother, the deputy sheriff of this small Eastern Shore town, was being forced to resign amid reports that he had purposely overlooked evidence crucial to this murder case. No official comment has been made by either the Wathen family or the school board, but privately friends are saying that Wathen had been despondent about the charges and the loss of his wife, and sources close to this investigation are saying that he left a suicide note in which he steadfastly maintained in his innocence. Wathen's death will effectively close the government's murder case. Meanwhile, the family of Elizabeth Bryson, Wathen's victim, issued a brief statement just a few moments ago expressing regret over the loss of life. Bryson left behind a husband and three young children, for whom coping with her death has been complicated by the fast-moving investigation and arrest of her former supervisor. As one resident put it, 'Perhaps now Michael Bryson and his family can get back to the business of grieving.' For both families, however, the answers to the mystery surrounding Bryson's death died when Wathen took his own life this afternoon. This is Andrea Carson, reporting live from Atlantic Hospital in Berlin, Maryland. Back to you in the studio."

I turned down the sound and sat heavily on the bunk.

"Isn't that unbelievable?" Wayne said.

"I don't know what to say. I feel awful, Wayne. I feel like I killed him."

His response was quick and forceful. "Oh no—don't you do that to yourself. You didn't kill anybody. He did."

"But if I hadn't called you—"

"Then your friend's murderer would have gotten away with it. Completely. And he might have gotten into a similar situation with another woman again. Would that have been better?"

"No," I admitted. "But this isn't what I wanted either. I never... I never thought he planned it."

There was a pause. Wayne's voice was curious when he spoke.

"So what changed? You seemed pretty sure it was murder when you called me."

I really wasn't sure what I was thinking. I had been so intent on Bernie's guilt—and I still was.

"I don't know—I just feel guilty that he died. I guess I saw it as an argument that maybe got out of hand, maybe he hit her and knocked her out, then got scared."

"So even if he did, fixing up her car so that it would drive off the bridge seems fairly premeditated to me," Wayne observed drily. "He wasn't exactly a Boy Scout, San."

"No, I know, you're right. Thanks, Wayne. Thanks for calling."

He could tell by my tone that he was being dismissed, but he maintained his good humor.

"Don't beat yourself up about this. Period. And don't be such a stranger," he said. "You know, I could do more for you than investigate stories."

"I'm sure," I said, smiling in spite of myself. "Goodnight."

"Night."

I ended the call and stared at the television. I didn't really feel guilty for Bernie's death. Even if he hadn't meant for it to end the way it had, he had hurt someone only to protect himself. No, I felt guilty because his death was a relief. I wouldn't have to testify. Michael and the children wouldn't be dragged through a long trial. For them at least, life could move on. But I suppose in the back of my mind I also knew that I now had no reason to see him again—and that bothered me more than I had expected.

I went back to my work, but now the sky was dark and the cockpit too cold to sit out. I gave in to morbid curiosity and watched every available news broadcast on every channel, but there was little new information. One station claimed that sources close to the investigation said additional evidence had been mounting, and they had even discovered tickets to St. Thomas purchased by Liz a few days before her death. It was speculated that she had planned for the couple to go public, and that Bernie had balked, leading to her murder. But of course, no one would know for sure.

The only two people who knew what went on in her car that night were dead.

I had just turned off the television and crawled into my berth when the phone rang again. I assumed it would be Wayne, and I really didn't want to talk to him, but on the other hand, if I didn't answer, he might worry about me. People tended to do that. I grabbed it without looking at the screen.

"Hello?"

There was a brief pause, a hesitation and intake of breath. I don't know why I was so certain, but I was.

"Michael?"

"Yeah, it's me," he said. "How did you know? This is a new number."

I thought about the reasons he would have for changing his phone number, and again I felt a pang of guilt.

"Lucky guess," I said as lightly as I could manage. "How are you?"

"Better, I guess. Did you hear about Wathen?"

"Yes. Tonight, on the news."

He sighed. "They called me right away. To make sure I was still in Pennsylvania. I guess it's a good thing I was."

"You're still staying with your parents?"

"Yes. The kids are doing so much better here." Michael paused a moment, then went on. "I don't think we're going to go back. They can't grow up in a place where everyone knows that their mother... where everyone knows what happened. That's really why I'm calling. I have an uncle who owns a paint factory outside of Morgantown. It's only about an hour from my parents' house. He has offered me a job as Executive Director of Finance."

"That's great," I said, trying to infuse my voice with a gladness I did not feel.

"It sounds like more than it is. The company's small—only about 250 employees. But I could live closer to my parents, and they could help with the children."

"It sounds like a good idea. Really."

There was another pause.

"I called to ask you a favor," he said finally.

"Sure."

"I have to go back and pack everything up, and I... I really don't want to go through her things. I guess I am almost afraid of what I might find. I don't have anyone else I trust to... I just don't want any more people involved in what happened than I have already. I'd be glad to pay you for your time."

"You don't have to pay me. I'd be glad to help," I said.

"I know it's a lot to ask. At least let me put you up in a hotel for a few nights."

"Sure, sounds fair."

"How is next weekend for you? I'm going down Thursday to clear up everything at work and meet with a realtor. It will probably take two or three days. I've already hired movers to come the third week in May."

"That sounds fine. I can be there Saturday morning and stay until Monday if that works for you," I said, mentally reorganizing the calls and meetings that remained in the week.

"Just so you know, I am going to stay in a hotel too," Michael said. "It will make it easier to pack things up if I'm not trying to live in the house, and to be honest, I just don't think I can stand sleeping there. I know it's stupid, but there you have it."

I wasn't sure what to say. The conversation felt stilted and awkward. The sense of closeness we developed during that brief, intense time together right after Liz's death had vanished. It felt like the maneuvering of a blind date.

"That would be great. Okay if I meet you at the house on Saturday around ten?"

"Right. See you then."

But his voice was left hanging, as if he had something more to say.

"Michael?" I asked.

There was a pause.

"You know, I am beginning to think I never really knew her at all," he added, so softly that I nearly missed the words. Then the signal went dead.

After the call ended I sat quietly for a while, thinking. I was honest enough to admit that a part of me hoped that the time together might amount to something, lead to something, while at the same time I knew that the odds were against it. He was crawling back into the family fold— he had already decided to move some six hours in the other direction, to a landlocked suburb of a West Virginia university town. It sounds shallow to say that my boat was more important to me than a relationship, but in fact, my boat was a relationship—the last remnants of a marriage that ended too soon. To even consider a future that might include giving it up was to consider giving up the dreams I had shared with Ryan, and that wasn't something I was ready to do.

I don't lie to myself often. I knew all of this, but I also knew that even the brief warmth of human contact with Michael Bryson felt good in a way that nothing had for a long time. If the only risk was disappointment, it was a risk I thought I might be willing to take. It felt better than the resignation I had been living with.

At least this was my state of mind as I interpreted it. Michael might not have known Liz, but I did not even know myself.

Chapter 15

I PULLED UP TO MICHAEL Bryson's house an hour before noon the following Saturday. The traffic had been a nightmare, and I sent a text warning I would be late.

Bayview looked as forlorn in the late spring as it had in March, with only the barest of green patches showing through the muddy earth. But the spindly trees all had leaves, and one of his neighbors had hung brightly colored plastic eggs from each tree and propped an inflatable bunny on a lawn chair out front, perhaps leaving them up well past Easter in defiance of the general melancholy. Hope is hard to kill.

Michael's car was already in the driveway, and the front door was open, with only the glass storm door closed. I tapped on the glass and then tried the handle, pulling it open a few inches and calling Michael's name.

"Back here!" he called.

I moved in the direction of the voice. I noted that the living room was packaged up in large cardboard cartons, taped, and labeled. It already had the empty look of a vacant house now that it was stripped of its photographs, candles, and pillows. Michael was in a small bedroom at the end of the hall, kneeling and surrounded by milk crates full of file folders and papers. He shrugged apologetically.

"This is the worst mess. Liz kept everything—every college paper, every lesson, every worksheet. I don't know what to do with all of this," Michael said, shaking his head.

"Why don't you let me go through it?" I suggested. "If it's something personal that you or the kids might want, I'll save it. If it looks like teaching material, we can box it up and drop it off at the school. Some other teacher might want it."

He rose at once, looking relieved.

"Great. I'll go work on the kids' rooms. Thank, San," he added, giving me a brief hug. "Thanks for coming."

"No problem," I said.

I settled in and began sorting. Michael was right. Liz saved everything. It wasn't long before I forgot about Michael in the other room, carefully wrapping his children's stuffed animals and baby dreams in plastic bubbles which would outlast the childhood that had spawned them. Instead, I found myself reading her junior year thesis on Chaucer's *Wife of Bath*, followed by her poetry portfolio, and it seemed that in no time at all an hour had gone by and I had put only a few papers in small stacks, insignificant beside the mound around me.

Somehow the fact of Liz's death made her every word important, noteworthy.

I looked at the clock, then listened for a moment. I heard the muffled movements of Michael as he sorted through the toy box across the hall. I looked at the remaining boxes, squared my shoulders, and attacked them with fervor. Another hour went by, then two. I had waded through file folder after file folder of lesson plans and neatly typed class sets of handouts. I had stopped careful perusing and had taken to quick, cursory glances at the first few sheets. I was starting to see the bottom of the pile, and this encouraged me. It was at this point that a long white legal envelope fluttered out and slipped to the floor. I picked it up curiously.

The envelope had been addressed to someone named Debra Windler, and the postmark was October 26 of last year. It was already opened, so I did not hesitate to pull out the contents.

The envelope contained a form letter from the Social Security Administration. It began:

Dear Ms. Windler:

Enclosed is the new Social Security card you requested. Please verify that the information on the card is correct. If any of the information on this card is incorrect, contact your local S.S.A. office at one of the locations listed on the back of this letter as soon as possible.

It went on to admonish Debra that her card was an important identification document and should be treated as such. The letter ended without a closing or signature—a typical government missive—and the bottom contained a torn perforation which had apparently contained the aforesaid card.

I turned the envelope over and looked again at the address. It was an apartment in Ocean City. Why would Liz have this letter? Why would she have kept it? Was it something she accidentally picked up with a stack of papers in a teachers' copy room? Was Debra a good friend?

I knew it probably meant nothing, but when someone has died suddenly, everything surrounding them is something of a mystery. I remember reading over Ryan's scrawled notes in our ship's log after his funeral as if I expected to find some secret message there, all the while knowing that a summary of engine work and oil changes was not likely to bring me any revelation about my husband's life or death. Still... I placed the envelope in the front of the topmost folder and resolved to be the one to stop by the school and seek out the opportunity to talk to Debra Windler.

Michael stood in the doorway and smiled tiredly.

"Ready for a break?"

"Absolutely. I'm almost done," I answered with a grin.

He looked around the room and nodded gratefully.

"This is great. It would have taken me a week. Did you find anything I should see?"

He stumbled a bit on the question. I thought about the envelope, but it didn't seem worth mentioning.

"No, teacher stuff. I'll drop it at the school, see if anyone wants it."

"Thanks." He sounded relieved. "I'm done in the kids' rooms. You want to give me a hand in the kitchen?"

I rose and went with him. We worked in the little kitchen for the remainder of the afternoon, no more than a few feet apart, our bodies often brushing as we stooped to put pots or pans in the cardboard boxes. Perhaps it was a natural reaction to the tension of the situation, but as we went on, things that would have seemed mundane and commonplace started to seem faintly amusing. There was a coffee canister full of pacifiers that Michael said had been lost for years and a cache of children's vitamins behind the microwave cart, obviously deposited by a reluctant child. At this last find, we both broke into laughter.

I was still laughing when I felt his gaze. We were both sitting on the floor, a few feet apart. I looked in his face, suddenly so serious and yet not quite sad. He smiled ruefully.

"I was just thinking... It sounds wrong to say, but I don't think I've ever really laughed in this house before today. You know, I went to work every day, I came home, I ate dinner, I played with the kids, but I can't remember laughing. Can that be right?"

I didn't answer. It wasn't that kind of question.

"I guess I always thought, you know, that even with the problems Liz was having, our marriage was pretty normal. How could I have thought that? That living for years without laughing was normal?" Michael shook his head.

"Every marriage has ups and downs," I said.

"I can't imagine you going for four years without laughing," he said, and suddenly it was electric between us.

I looked at the floor. "After Ryan died... I stopped laughing. So I guess this is a good experience for both of us."

That remark carried more portent than I had intended. The words left my mouth and fell heavily between us. I don't know if he was looking at me or not, because I was staring intently at the linoleum while a flush crept into my face.

He got up and moved to the counter under the pretense of taping a carton. A few minutes passed while I finished with the box beside me. By the time I felt able to look up, the moment had passed.

Michael looked at his watch.

"It's almost four thirty. San, I'm sorry—you never had lunch. "

I shrugged. "I wasn't hungry."

"Well, I'm starving. Why don't we call it quits and go get something to eat? I already checked into the hotel, so I have both our keys. Do you mind driving? My car is already loaded with the kids' clothes."

I agreed, and we set off. We decided again on downtown O.C., where we were more likely to have anonymity, although we didn't say it out loud. It was prime spring convention season, and the resort town was currently hosting an association of Maryland government retirees some 10,000 strong. Michael had made reservations at an inexpensive motel on the mainland side of the bridge because every decent hotel room along the coast was booked. We decided to stop there and drop off my bag before we went to dinner.

The motel was a white clapboard, three story colonial that served as an office and diner, flanked on both sides by long, brick one-story buildings so nondescript as to be positively inconspicuous. Every room had a curtained widow, a white door, and a plastic lawn chair. Michael directed me to the parking space in front of room 103 and handed me a key.

"You're in 104. My stuff is already in 103," he said. "Do you want to shower or anything before dinner?"

"Is that a hint?" I asked in an attempt to ease the tension. Our ride over had been limited to uncomfortable small talk, and I had finally turned on the radio to fill in the silences.

He pretended to hold his nose. "Definitely."

"I think I will take a quick shower. I can be ready in twenty minutes. Is that okay?"

"Sure. Uh..."

He paused as I opened my door.

"What?"

"Just so you know. I don't want you to get the wrong idea. The rooms are adjoining. It was all they had left."

If I cherished any thoughts that fit into the "wrong idea" category, I suppose this was a warning. I adopted a casual tone.

"Not a problem. Just knock first."

Once inside, I saw that the door was not only substantial but also included both a handset and deadbolt lock.

No wrong ideas there.

I showered gratefully, thankful for the time alone. Twenty minutes later I was dressed in fresh jeans, my short hair toweled dry. My makeup routine consisted of faint blush on the cheeks and, if I was really trying to impress someone, a little mascara. I put on mascara and knocked on the connecting door.

A lock turned and Michael opened it, hair damp and looking somehow very young.

"Ready to go?" he asked.

"Ready."

I noted without meaning to that he left the door between our rooms open as we left.

We had a few beers and a pleasant dinner at a bayside bar and grill. The occasional awkwardness we felt was dulled by alcohol, and I found myself having a really nice time. Michael talked about his new job and his children, and I talked about a couple I was helping to get their deposit back from a contract they had on a house after the inspection turned up several undisclosed problems.

No one talked about Liz.

He offered to drive my car back to the motel, and I let him. I had only had two beers, just a warm buzz really, but it felt good to have someone else in charge, even if only for a few minutes. He walked me to my door and then stopped. I felt him bend toward me, and I raised my face. His eyes were serious as he kissed me. Our lips touched, then pressed and opened. I closed my eyes.

He drew back.

"Good night," he said.

And he was gone, slipping into his room before I opened my eyes.

I don't know how long I stood there, but by the time I got out my key and opened my own room, the door to Michael's room was closed.

I didn't try the knob.

Chapter 16

I FELL INTO BED AFTER only the briefest of showers, and I slept a dreamless slumber. I woke when the early morning sunlight brightened the room to an unbearable whiteness, having inexplicably left the heavy drapes wide open.

I took a long, hot shower, replaying the night before, the kiss. Somewhere between shampoo and conditioner, I realized I had no idea what came next.

My cell phone was ringing as I turned off the shower. I grabbed a towel and lunged for the dresser. Michael's number.

"Hey," I said breathlessly.

"We still have the attic and the garage, but that's it," he said, voice happy and buoyant. "Are you ready for breakfast?"

"Sure," I said, ignoring the water dripping from my body to the carpet. "Where to?"

"Let's cruise the strip and look for a buffet," he suggested.

"Sure."

"Fifteen minutes okay?"

"Sure."

It seemed to be the only word I could utter. As soon as I ended the call I dried off and threw on last night's jeans and a white long-sleeved t-shirt. I combed my wet hair, added blush and mascara, and viewed myself critically. I think I am attractive—even after Ryan, there have certainly been men who signaled they were attracted to me. I have olive skin that looks tanned even in the winter, dark eyes, and a heart-shaped face. My body has the lean, muscled look of someone who goes to the gym, and I do, religiously, three days a week. But the stress of Ryan's death marked my eyes with a web of fine lines, and my once long, brown hair is now cut short, and streaked with shades of blonde to cover the early gray. Even with that, I know I look younger than my thirty-five years. Attractive, yes. Competent, professional-looking even, but not pretty. That had never bothered me until now. Michael knocked on the outer door. He was clad in khakis and a clean, powder blue shirt, and he was smiling.

"Ready?"

"Absolutely." I answered his smile with my own and made a concerted effort to stop thinking.

We climbed in the car and headed down Ocean Highway.

About half of the restaurants were not yet open for the season, which officially started with Memorial Day. Michael pulled into a pancake house on 46th street and we went in. The place was semi-packed, with a mix of conventioneers in vacation clothes and church folk just out of mid-morning service. We were only two, so we were seated within minutes. We placed an order and the waiter, clearly a college student, brought us coffee which he promptly spilled on the vinyl cloth and splashed on Michael's chest. As the waiter mopped ineffectively at the table and Michael went to the restroom to try to rescue his shirt, I happened to glance to the right. Betty Ann Oriwitz of the impossibly purple dress was seated at the next table, this time clad in turquoise.

I don't know what prompted me. I stood up and reached over, touching her arm.

"Betty Ann," I said, smiling warmly. "How are you?"

She looked at me blankly. Everyone at her table—husband, friend, several children—stared at me as well.

"Sandra Beck. We met at Liz Bryson's funeral."

I pushed on, driven by something I could not define.

"I'm helping Liz's husband pack up her things, and we've run across a lot of teaching materials. Is it okay if I drop them off Monday morning on my way home? They might be helpful to someone."

Now that I had appropriately categorized myself, Betty Ann beamed.

"Miz Beck! I'm so sorry, I didn't recognize you at first. I wasn't expectin' to see you here. Mr. Bryson, nice to see you."

Michael cleared his throat behind me.

"I was telling Betty Ann that you had some of Liz's teaching materials that someone might be able to use," I explained.

Michael nodded and was about to say something when the waiter called him over with a question about our order. He excused himself and walked back to the table.

"Sure, hon." Betty Ann smiled warmly at me. "You just drop it on by. We have a box or two from her file cabinet of personal things you can pick up at the same time."

I thanked her and started to turn away. Then I had a thought.

"Oh, and there's some stuff for a Debra Windler. Is she still at your school?"

There was a palpable silence. Betty Ann looked almost physically pained.

"Honey, Debra Windler was a student some... I don't know, give or take twelve years ago. Long before Liz taught there. She was killed in an accident in her senior year. I don't know how Liz would have ended up with her things."

I didn't know how to respond.

"Well, honey, you just bring that stuff on by and we'll figger it out," Betty Ann said when I offered no other explanation.

"Thanks." I smiled weakly and went back to our table. Michael was looking at me intently. It was obvious he had heard the exchange.

"What was that about?" he asked quietly when Betty Ann's attention was focused back on her own brood.

"Nothing. Just an envelope I found."

"That belonged to a dead student? You didn't mention it yesterday."

Somewhere, in the very back of my mind where ideas I should forget (but don't) usually lodge, I had a vague feeling of disquiet. I couldn't explain it, and it certainly wasn't something to share.

I shrugged.

"I didn't know then that it belonged to a dead student. I thought it something of another teacher's."

"So how did Liz end up with it?"

"You know how schools are. The stuff was probably misfiled and ended up in Liz's cabinet. It could have been there for twelve years. It's no big deal."

Michael looked at me closely, then nodded. He relaxed a little.

"Sorry. I'm still a little edgy, I guess. I think I almost expected we'd find something... you know, that explained everything. I don't know, a journal or a letter. I started seeing the pastor at my parents' church when I first went home. He said I was waiting for an apology, and that I needed to stop looking for one." He shook his head ruefully. "I guess he was right."

The waiter brought our food then, and we avoided any other personal conversation. We finished breakfast and drove back to Michael's house. Very little remained to pack up, and it was done by mid-afternoon. The sun was bright and the air warm even for May. We loaded everything into a U-Haul trailer except the few cartons of teaching materials, which we put in my trunk. Then he went back to lock up. His face was a mixture of regret and relief.

"So now what?" I asked.

"I don't know. I have to hang around till tomorrow. I have to meet with the realtor tomorrow morning, and you were going to the school. Do you want to go to the beach? It's a great day for it."

Neither of us had brought a suit, but we both had shorts and t-shirts. We stopped at the hotel, grabbed two towels, and then stopped at a convenience store for sunscreen. Michael went in and came out with a Frisbee and some snacks.

The afternoon reminded me, when I thought of it later, of Sundays when I was seven or eight, and I went with my parents to the shore. It carried that same odd mix of the temporal and the endless—sky and beach stretching infinitely, but time ticking down to Monday morning and the alarm for school. Without saying it, we purposed to forget everything—Liz's death, our past lives, the responsibility for his children that Michael carried—and instead we tumbled about like children, tossing the disk and walking knee deep in the waves. We lingered on the beach until the sun dropped behind the tall concrete hotels, and we left it slowly, sand in our shoes. Still dressed in our beach clothes, we grabbed a quick dinner and had a few glasses of wine at a boardwalk tavern, then started back to the hotel.

"Do you want a bottle of wine?" Michael asked, slowing in front of a liquor store.

"Um... do you?"

He grinned, the first honest-to-goodness grin I'd seen from him. .

"Unequivocally, yes."

When he went inside, I sat in the car and tried to organize my thoughts. I had a sense that something had shifted between us during the day, though I wasn't sure what it was. This day felt like a date—not a first date, but the comfortable kind of date that you have once you know each other. It's just a bottle of wine, I reminded myself. But the combination of closing out this chapter of his life and staying in a motel room next to a single woman—I felt like I could see where this was going. I was afraid one or both of us would be sorry in the morning.

Michael got back in the car and we headed toward the motel. He tried to talk a little in the same light tone he had been using, but I couldn't shake my own stiff awkwardness brought on by my prediction of what was to come. When I didn't respond, he turned up the radio and beat out the tune on the steering wheel. As we pulled in front of our rooms, he switched it off.

"What's wrong?" he asked. "And don't say nothing. You haven't talked for ten minutes."

So much for that lie. I squeezed my knee to ground myself as I spoke.

"I just need to know what we're doing," I said. "Where is this going?"

"Where do you want it to go?" he asked, shifting so that he faced me.

This is where women are trained to be coy. Don't stick your neck out. The best answer in this situation is "I don't know." But that isn't what I said.

"I think I could fall in love with you."

He looked surprised, but he did not pull back. "Okay. Is that a bad thing?"

"I don't know. A lot has happened to you."

"So you think this is—what, a rebound thing? I am only attracted to you because my wife was killed?"

He didn't look hurt or angry. He looked like he really wanted to know.

"I don't know. Maybe. Are you?"

He touched my chin with his hand, bringing my eyes up to meet his.

"No. That isn't what this is about. Maybe the timing isn't great, but I know how I feel."

He leaned toward me, but I leaned away, my eyes searching his face.

"I don't want to get involved and then have you walk away."

Michael brushed the hair from my forehead tenderly.

"I promise I will not walk away."

He kissed me. It was soft, deep, and sweet. He drew back and breathed in, then exhaled audibly.

"I won't push you. If you don't want this, tell me."

"I want this," I said.

We got out of the car slowly and turned toward my room. I fumbled with the key, finally opening it, and we went in. He sat the wine on the bathroom counter while I rummaged in my bag for a corkscrew—I am nothing if not prepared—and then he poured it into the Styrofoam hotel coffee cups. As we drank, I saw us in the mirror, surrounded by shadows. Then Michael turned off the light.

The details of what happened next do not matter. It is enough to say that we made love.

I think now that it meant different things to both of us, but that did not make it any less important. For me, it was a like setting a deadline on my widowhood, my grief. I do not know what it was for Michael, but I suspect it was a kind of vindication. I remember thinking, fleetingly, as I burrowed in his embrace, that it was good that this had happened between us, two adults who had known pain and loss. Life owed us something, some happiness.

A foolish cliché, really. Life never owes us anything at all.

Chapter 17

IT WAS RAINING, SO MORNING came slowly, in degrees of graying light. I woke first, and I lay there listening to Michael's soft, even breathing. He had set the alarm for seven o'clock, and it was barely six, but I couldn't go back to sleep. I found myself watching the minutes tick off, snuggling into the warmth of the bed and the presence of another body beside me.

When the alarm finally went off, Michael rolled over and hugged me.

"Hey," he said.

"Hey."

"You okay?" he asked.

"Mmm hmm."

He hugged me again and kissed the top of my head, then rolled out of bed, stretching.

"I need to get on the road pretty early to beat the traffic around D.C. I'll probably leave right after I meet with the realtor. Are you going to take that stuff to the school?"

I nodded. "They had some other things of Liz's, remember? What do you want me to do with those?"

There was a pause. Her name, which had gone largely unspoken between us in the past twenty-four hours, drove an almost visible wedge between us. He paused, looking away.

"Why don't you look through it," he said offhandedly, suddenly engrossed in the cable ad on top of the T.V. "It's probably nothing, just school-related papers. If you think I should keep anything, you can mail it to me. I'll leave you the address. If there's anything…else, call me."

"Sure," I said evenly as he walked into his room and started the shower. I don't know what I expected, but this dismissal was not it.

I got up, showered, and changed. I was ready to go in no more than ten minutes. When Michael came back in, rubbing his wet hair with a towel, he looked surprised.

"You get ready faster than any woman I've ever met."

I smiled with what I hoped was a bland expression.

"It's my gift."

"Look, I'm not really sure… what I mean is, I just can't make any kind of plans right now."

"Walking away after all?" I asked, the hurt creeping like a traitor into my voice.

"I know. This is coming out wrong." Michael ran his hands through his hair, frustrated. "I guess what I'm trying to say is that I would like this to be something, I'd like to see you again. I just don't know when, and I don't want you to feel like I was dishonest with you."

He was clearly upset. I softened and reached for his hand.

"I don't expect anything. If something works out, great. If it doesn't, I won't lie to you, Michael, I'll be disappointed. But I won't be sorry. Okay?"

He looked into my eyes and smiled.

"Okay."

We hugged for a few minutes and then Michael wrote down the address of the house he was renting, folded it, and put it in my purse. He walked me out to the car, still barefoot.

"I'll call you," he said, leaning over to kiss me goodbye.

"No promises necessary," I said, but I didn't mean it, and we both knew it.

I drove to the school, firmly putting any thoughts about the future out of my mind. It was on the southern side of Pineyfield, perhaps ten minutes from Main Street. I located the visitor parking spots near the flagpole. It was after eight a.m., and classes must have already started, because the parking lot was full of cars and one sleepy-looking student was straggling toward the building. The school itself was a long, brick institution whose recent renovation seemed to have been limited to a front archway and a large white sign proudly pronouncing "The Home of the Ospreys." I walked through the front door and into a glass-windowed office. It looked enough like a prison that I expected to be buzzed in, but the door was unlocked. A woman in late middle-age with an unusually tall beehive hairdo reminiscent of the fifties looked up from the stack of papers on her desk.

"May I help you?"

"Yes. My name is Sandra Beck. I spoke to Betty Ann Oriwitz about dropping off some teaching materials and picking up some boxes that had belonged to Elizabeth Bryson."

That name seemed to cause physical pain. The woman winced and picked up the phone.

"Betty Ann, I have a woman here who says she is supposed to pick up something of Elizabeth Bryson's....Where? Behind the paper cabinet? No, I can get it. She also says she has some things to drop off. Do you really think—all right....No, I'll take care of her. All right, Betty Ann. Mmm hmm."

She got off the phone and rose, fixing me with a disapproving stare.

"I'll call for a student to get the boxes. There's just the two, and they're in the machine room. Do you need someone to carry in the things you are dropping off?"

"If it's not too much trouble," I said, feeling like I had committed some unforgivable breach of high school etiquette.

She didn't answer me, but disappeared into a long corridor that opened at the wall behind her desk.

I stood in the office awkwardly, watching the second hand on the clock. When she didn't return, I decided to kill time by walking back out to the main hall and looking at the display cases.

The first case was full of trophies and team pictures, some going back fifty years. The second contained framed photographs of teachers and students accepting awards and pieces of student artwork. I was struck suddenly by a picture in the bottom corner of a young female student posing with a giant check representing a college scholarship. On one side stood a beaming Bernie Wathen, and on the other, hand on the girl's shoulder and looking directly into the camera, was Liz.

I was amazed that the photo remained here—a suicidal suspected murderer and his alleged victim, not exactly a school's proudest moment. I suppose the display case was just part of the background here, and no one but me had even glanced at the display case in years. As I leaned over to get a closer look, I was also struck by how different Liz appeared compared to the woman I remembered. She had lost so much weight that she was at the point of being bone-thin, and her round face had become oval with an angular, definitive chin. I always thought she was pretty, but here she reminded me of a diamond: hard and sharp.

"Miss Beck." The secretary's commanding voice jolted me from behind. I straightened, embarrassed, as if I had been caught where I did not belong. She stood behind me with a stern expression. Beside her were two teen-aged boys, each carrying a large cardboard box.

"These boys will take the boxes out to your car and pick up what you have."

"Great," I said, offering her my most charming smile.

The woman turned away and opened the office door.

"Good day."

The door closed.

I looked at the boys, who seemed embarrassed.

"Thanks a lot, guys. I'm right out front."

They didn't speak, but carried the boxes to my car and sat them on the ground, watching as I opened the hatch. We exchanged the cartons of teaching materials from Michael's house with Liz's things, and then they were gone.

It was a silent, sterile exchange, and somehow it made me sad.

Chapter 18

I NAVIGATED MY WAY TO the interstate and started the long drive home. Perhaps it was the rain, but I wanted quiet, and the hours ahead in the car were an opportunity to slow time and assess what was happening in my life. Thus far I had managed not to think about last night, or (to be honest) not to dwell on it when it slipped like a thief into my consciousness. Now I wanted to think about it, to consider it, to turn it over in my mind, look at the possibilities. No matter how much we fool ourselves into thinking that sex can be just sex, it never is.

We women are all romantics under the skin. Too many Disney movies as children, where we are all princesses and we live to be earned, won, cherished, loved. I had been fortunate to have a fairytale relationship once, and against all of my better judgement, I found myself beginning to believe that it might be possible to have something like it again.

Naïve optimism must be a survival instinct of the human heart.

I was about an hour into weighing out the possible pitfalls of a relationship that began with a woman's death when the phone rang. It was a referral from another client, and the caller sounded like she needed more attention than I could give while driving in the rain. I was just a few miles outside of a town, so I promised to call her back in five minutes and started looking for a place to pull in. I spotted the golden arches through the driving rain and parked, then dialed her back.

It was the kind of story I hear a lot. The woman's elderly father, who suffered from dementia, had written a check for $2,800 to a wholesale meat salesman who had come to his door. This had caused his next two rent checks to bounce, and now the senior condominium complex where he lived was threatening to evict him. When she realized what was happening, she had gone to the condo manager, but while he was sympathetic, he still wanted the rent. She tried to contact the salesman at the number on the card he left with her father, but he never returned her calls. She didn't know the name of the company. Yes, she tried the police, but while they agreed that $2800 was an exorbitant price for fifty pounds of ground beef, it did not constitute a crime or warrant an investigation. Now she was stuck paying her father's rent, which she could barely afford. Could I help?

I promised her I would do what I could and agreed to charge her only if I was able to get the money returned. By the time I had written down all of the details and gotten off the line, the rain had stopped. My mouth was watering from the aroma of French fries that permeated the interior of my car, and rationalizing that I needed to get out and stretch anyway, I went inside to grab lunch.

Sometimes the most trivial decisions can start in motion a chain of unfortunate events. When I got back out to the car, the rain had ended, and I was feeling uncomfortably full. I decided to walk around a bit more before getting back in the car, and in doing so, I saw the boxes.

What was the point of dragging them to the boat? It was unlikely that Liz had anything in her school desk worth keeping, but I could take a quick look now, and if not, there was a dumpster right here in the parking lot. I opened the hatch, slid the first box to the edge, and opened it.

Inside was a jumble that consisted mainly of the cheesy gifts parents buy for teachers: apple paperweights, post-it notes with grammar jokes, a desk calendar with 365 days of creative bulletin board ideas. There were cards, too, for Teacher Appreciation Day and Christmas, and a cardboard Teacher of the Year Award from one of her classes. Not much, really, to show for all of those hours spent in the classroom, all of those nights of grading papers. I carried it to the dumpster.

The second box must have come from Liz's file cabinet. It was filled with hanging folders neatly marked in felt-tip pen: "Professional," "Parent Correspondence," "Workshops." At the bottom of were two unmarked folders that contained miscellaneous bits and pieces: receipts for supplies, articles torn from educational journals, a recipe from a parent for Oreo truffles, a clipping of a miracle diet from a women's magazine. I was about to close the box when I saw the edge of a manila envelope at the back of the last folder. I pulled it out and opened it, glancing inside: some letters and opened envelopes. Probably all parent-teacher correspondence, but I dumped them out just to be sure. I flipped over the top envelope and froze. It was addressed to Debra Windler.

I opened it slowly.

>Le Vrae University
>34561 Mason Blvd.
>Detroit, Michigan 33298

>Dear Ms. Debra Windler:

>Congratulations on your recent completion of our paralegal program. Your excellent academic record is a testament to your hard work and the commitment you have to obtaining a college education. Should you desire to continue your education by completing a degree in legal studies, please be aware that we offer a Bachelor of Science in Legal Studies through our School of Distance Learning. One of our trained academic advisers would be happy to discuss this option and others available for adult professionals by phone at 735-555-9084.

>We wish you the best of luck with your future plans.

>Sincerely,

>Randall Vines
>Dean
>LU School of Distance Learning

The letter was undated, but the envelope was stamped from Le Vrae, and the postmark read January eighteenth of this year. The address was the same as the social security letter I had read in Michael's house.

A teenager who had been dead for years was suddenly receiving mail and taking classes, and all of the letters ended up in Liz's possession. I may not be a genius, but this was looking, as Alice would have said, "curiouser and curiouser."

I rummaged through the other letters quickly. All of them were addressed to Debra Windler. One was a credit card statement. The other was a bank statement. Debra Windler had had a balance of $3,803.00 in her savings account and $136.17 in her checking account as of the first of March.

It looked as if Liz had been using the dead girl's name as a second identity—perhaps in preparation to run away with Bernie. The problem was that setting up bank accounts and completing a paralegal accreditation program were not impulsive, spontaneous acts. These were well-thought-out plans for a new life, and they did not jive with the portrait that the *Washington Post* and the federal government had painted of the emotionally vulnerable victim of Bernie Wathen.

I stared at the small stack in my hands. I did not for a moment pretend this was not a significant find. The question was what I was going to do about it.

I could walk over to the big green dumpster and throw this box and all of its contents away. This would hurt no one. Liz was dead. Bernie was dead. Her motives, even her sanity, were moot at this point.

I could call Michael or send them to him. They would undoubtedly cause additional pain, re-open a wound that had only just scabbed over, and prove to him yet again how little he knew his wife and how his marriage had been over long before Liz's car had plunged off the Assateague Bridge.

And then there was me. With my innate sense of justice, my insertion of myself into the situation surrounding Liz's death, I had been instrumental in Bernie's arrest. I had not seen or heard any evidence suggesting Bernie knew about this second identity. According to him, they had made no serious plans for a future together. Of course, he could have been lying, and they may have made an elaborate escape plan, only to have him back out at the last minute. Certainly that was a scenario that could have led to a fight and Liz's murder.

There was another possibility as well. Perhaps Liz had been living some kind of double life that was symptomatic of a more profound psychological disturbance than Michael or her doctors had recognized. In that case, there may have been multiple affairs, and a far more tangled trail of deceit than the one Wayne Kremm uncovered in his story.

The bottom line is that knowing these answers wouldn't matter. They wouldn't change a thing.

Disposing of the whole mess would be the kind thing to do. For everyone.

That is not what I did.

I wanted to know to the truth, I was burning to know it. I was possessed by a kind of morbid curiosity about the woman who had shared Michael's bed before me, the woman who had given birth to his children. I wasn't going to be able to let it go. I guess the bottom line was that I wanted to prove to myself that Liz had fully intended to leave him, that she would have been just as gone if her body had not floated out from under the Assateague Bridge. In some convoluted logic, that would mean that our relationship, if it existed, was not bound to her death.

I have said before that I am good at what I do. In the process of helping my clients I have become skilled at wheedling information from the unlikeliest of sources. I knew I could check at the mailbox, the bank, and the credit card company, and if there was anything to find, any more evidence, one way or the other of Liz's intentions before her death, I could find it. It was what I did.

That platitude, "The truth shall make you free"? I had enough experience to know that the truth often screws you up, makes you miserable. I have seen the truth ruin people's lives. But in this case, whatever I found, I didn't have to share it. Unless I thought it would help provide some closure or comfort to Michael or his children, I could keep it to myself.

I was good at that, too.

Of course, every action has consequences. In my line of work I should know that better than most.

I got in the car and typed the address on the LeVrae envelope into my phone's GPS. Then I turned the car around and headed back toward Ocean City.

Chapter 19

THE 134TH STREET ADDRESS WAS not an apartment at all, but a block-long strip mall surrounded by high-rise condos and vacation townhouses. The actual street address—2008—belonged to a small shipping store which went by the whimsical title of "Post It."

I considered what to say when I went in. There might be additional mail, waiting to be retrieved, but I couldn't think of a scenario in which they would give it to me. Of course, there might be nothing anyway, and she could have closed out the box before her death. Then again, if she was planning some sort of second life with Bernie as Debra Windler, wasn't it possible she left a forwarding address for the place she hoped to be? Was there perhaps an apartment on some island somewhere, a hibiscus in the window, gathering dust, and a landlord wondering why that nice couple had never shown up?

Legally, none of this information could be given to me. It was private, protected. On the other hand, there is no limit to the transgressions that can be committed unwittingly by underpaid and undereducated minimum wage workers. I brushed my short hair, applied some blush in the rear view mirror, and tried hard to look reputable.

The store itself consisted of two rows of small mailboxes and a counter, flanked on either side by displays of brown wrapping paper, wide packing tape, and bags of Styrofoam "peanuts." A young man with an advanced case of terminal acne stood behind the counter. His name tag bore the name "Keith." He didn't smile.

"Hi!" I said cheerily, putting on a higher voice and the best blonde imitation possible for someone mostly brunette. "I feel sooo stupid, but I'm in town on vacation? And I'm looking for a friend of mine?"

I've noticed that most young women phrase everything in the form of a question, as if they expected to be on Jeopardy at any moment, so I thought I'd throw this in as a distraction. The boy blinked.

"Does she work here?"

"No!" I laughed good naturedly. "This was the address on all her cards and stuff, and I thought, you know, since I was in town? I'd surprise her? Only this isn't a real address, you know? So where do I go?"

The boy seemed to grasp this and pulled out a small file box.

"What's your friend's name?"

"Deb. Deb Windler."

He turned the three-by-five cards laboriously, one at a time, while I tried to maintain the appropriate grateful and dimwitted expression.

"Aw, man, that's too bad."

"What?" I asked striving to keep the edge from my voice.

"She closed out her box in March. No forwarding address. I can't help you, out, man."

I managed to keep my face blank.

"Bummer," I said with what I hoped was a vacant smile.

"You know... Cathy maybe could help you. She's the one who took the cancellation order," the boy said, clearly racking his brain for some useful information. "She's in the back. Do you want me to get her?"

"Yeah... sure, why not? I came all this way, you know? I'd really like to see her."

Keith disappeared for several minutes and a middle-aged woman reappeared in his place. My spirits fell. She had the look of management.

"Keith says you're trying to locate someone and this is their last known address?"

I immediately adjusted my role.

"Yes. An old friend. I haven't seen her in years, but this was the address on her Christmas card, and I'd hate to miss her if I'm in town."

The woman nodded.

"I'm afraid we can't help you. She closed her account in March. I took the order myself. Said she'd had enough of this weather. She didn't leave any forwarding address, said she'd notify everyone herself. I remember because that's unusual. Everyone leaves an address. But as far as I know, we never got another piece of first-class mail for her, so I guess she did."

My disappointment was tangible.

"I'm sorry, honey," the woman said more sympathetically. "But you know, you might want to try over at the Racquet club. There's a hairdresser's upstairs there, and I know that's where she got her hair done, because I saw her there."

'You saw Debra at the hairdresser's?"

"Sure. Goin' blonde, sometime in March after she closed her account. I was surprised, you know, because she said she was leaving town. And it was real late at night, too—maybe seven-thirty or thereabouts, and the salon is usually closed. I was working out, but I know the only one working was Marcie because I stopped up there to make an appointment when I saw the lights on. Marcie was cutting her hair and coloring it, so she might could help you."

I thanked the woman and headed for the car.

It was starting to look more and more like Liz had intended to run away with Bernie at the time of her death. The hair color was something of a surprise, though. When had she become a blonde? No one had mentioned this in anything I had heard, either from Michael, at the funeral, or in the many newscasts. I determined to wrestle the truth from Marcie, even if it cost me a haircut.

The Racquet Club and Gym was actually just a few blocks down from the strip mall on the bayside. It was a squat, brick building set at the back of a huge parking lot. It was older and did not have the wide, floor-length windows of most modern gyms. It had several tennis courts on one side and a section of atrium which was probably the indoor pool and a small, single glass door as an entrance. I parked by the courts and went inside.

The lobby was done in a nondescript gray without artwork or other ornamentation, and perfumed with the strong smell of chlorine and sweat. Eighties rock was being pumped in all around me, just loud enough to take the place of conversation. In the distance were several doors to the locker rooms and a corridor which announced that it led to the exercise room and the pool. This area was securely blocked by a large counter stacked with clean white towels and clipboards. A big man in perhaps his thirties, wearing a muscle shirt and drinking a V-8, smiled welcomingly, and the music dropped a notch. His tanned skin glistened under the ceiling light as if it had been oiled.

"Hey! How you doin' today?"

He said it so warmly that I at first thought I must know him. Then I realized that he thought I was one of the members. In a vacation town like this one, hundreds of condo owners probably joined but only visited a few weekends a year.

"Hi." I smiled back. "I'm looking for the hairdresser's?"

"Oh." He nodded, smile temporarily abandoned. "Upstairs."

He motioned to his left, then turned back to a television that hung on one corner of the wall, tuned to ESPN and muted so that the action was a silent ballet to the stereo playing. I followed his directions to a set of circular stairs, wrought iron and brass, in the corner of the lobby. A sign on the wall announced that the bar, the machine room, and Shears could be found at the top of the stairs. Shears sounded promising, so I went up.

The beauty salon was actually much nicer than the gym would have led me to expect. It had wide French doors painted white, and the interior was sponge-painted in soft blues and grays. There was a reception area with a long gilt table and a high-backed chair. Along the walls were several cushioned loveseats and baskets of magazines. The remainder of the salon was curtained of by a thick brocade tapestry. It did not look like the sort of place a Pineyfield local would frequent—it had vacation money written all over it.

A tone had sounded at my entrance and an attractive woman appeared. She had tastefully frosted hair and perfect make-up and wore a slim, blue silk pants suit. I immediately felt frumpy.

"May I help you?"

I made a split second decision that this woman was not going to tell me anything outright. She already had more self-confidence than I did, and I hadn't even asked the first question. I decided to try a more circumspect approach.

"I'd like to get a haircut."

She surveyed me critically, as if determining how much damage existed to undo.

"Do you have an appointment?"

"No. I'm in town on vacation, and a friend of mine recommended you. Do you have time for a walk-in?"

She almost visibly shuddered at the term "walk-in."

"I believe I can work you in. We actually don't open for another half-hour, but since I'm here early... What is your name?"

I gave her my first name which she wrote in a small leather-bound book. She then introduced herself as Marcie and motioned me to come back.

"Who did you say your friend was?" she asked as she led me to the rear of the shop where the sinks stood.

I took a shot. "Debra Windler."

She turned and glanced at me. "Really?"

"You seem surprised."

"I am," she said, getting out a smock and fitting it over my shoulders.

"Why?" I asked as she pushed my chair back and turned on the water.

"Let me know if this is too hot. Well, because I only did her hair one time, and that was at least two months ago. She's never been back. I wondered if perhaps it had been too drastic for her."

"Drastic?"

"The color change. Her hair had been so dark, and to go blonde, it can be an adjustment. And on top of the length change…"

"I think she may be away," I said helpfully. "We're old friends, but we don't get together often since I live on the western shore. I just happened to be in the area, and I stopped to see her, but she apparently has been out of town a while."

The woman nodded. "That would explain it, then. To be honest, I was a little offended. She came in at closing and I stayed late to do her. I don't know if she told you, but someone had just butchered her hair. Very short, very uneven. She told me she had actually been wearing a wig for two weeks, and I believe it. It was the worst haircut I've ever seen, and I am usually not one for talking down my competition. She said she was desperate, that she had a business trip to New York the next day, and could I do something. Do you usually use conditioner? Your hair is very dry. So, I gave her a cute cut, really flattered her face, and then she looked and me at asked if I could do her hair color just like mine. It was already seven o'clock—we close at seven—but she seemed so concerned about this trip, and I didn't have any plans that night, so I went ahead. I guess I'm a sucker for a sob story." I heard rather than saw her smile. "There we go, hold the towel and follow me."

The walls of the main salon were hung with photographs of the latest hairstyles, all of which resembled porcupines. I followed her to the chair where she lifted me to the appropriate height and swung me to face the mirror.

"What are we having done?"

"Just a trim," I said quickly, imagining myself shaved and bristling.

Marcie nodded and began to comb out my hair.

"You have a nice short cut, and a good face for it," she said. "So did Debra. That thin face, it looks good with short hair. Well, I'm glad to hear that she has been gone. She seemed so pleased with the color and everything. Really, she looked like a different person."

"I wish I had seen it. You know, it's funny, I talked to her on the phone just before Easter and she didn't mention the color change. I guess she wanted it to be a surprise. Do you remember when you did her hair?"

"Late March, I think. It may have been earlier." She stopped, snipped, stopped again. "It was earlier. I remember because I was even later getting home because of the rescue vehicles. I live out toward Assateague, and the Coast Guard and everyone else were out there looking for the body of that teacher."

I sat very still.

"Did you say," my voice came out hoarse, "did you say you did Debra's hair on the same night that the teacher was killed?"

Marcie nodded, intent on layering one side of my hair. "Mmhmm. I guess you saw it on the news. Wasn't that something? "

"You said you did her hair around seven?"

"The color took a while. I didn't finish till, oh, at least eight. Is everything all right?"

She had finally noticed my pallor.

"Fine," I lied.

I don't think I spoke for the remainder of the haircut. I felt like I was on the top of a building looking down a hundred sets of spiral stairs. My head was spinning and I felt sick to my stomach. I struggled to regain my composure as she chatted on, covering a wide variety of topics and seemingly oblivious to my discomfort. There were a few blessed moments of silence as she blew dry my hair. Then she unfastened the smock and smiled.

"How's that?"

In spite of everything, I had to admit that it was great haircut.

We went to the front desk where she wrote up a receipt, and I racked my brain for a way to get additional information. I thought of it just as I handed her the tip.

"By the way, is Debra still driving that little sports car? What was it, a Miata?" I asked offhandedly.

Marcie shrugged, and there was a trace of suspicion in her eyes. "I don't know. Why?"

"Oh, she was always complaining about it and said she might sell it. I always loved that car. I was actually thinking of making her an offer," I said.

This answer must have sounded reasonable, because the suspicion was gone. "I don't know," she said again. "She was driving a rental car that night. I walked out with her, and I noticed, because it was one of those big sedans, and she didn't seem like the sedan type, if you know what I mean."

"How did you know it was a rental car?" I asked.

"It had those Enterprise license plates. Maybe her Miata wasn't dependable enough to take to the airport."

"Probably not. I guess the closest commercial airport is up by Wilmington."

Marcie shook her head, "No, she was headed all the way to BWI. I remember because she said she had a nonstop shuttle from there to New York City, and she was going to get out early to beat traffic across the bridge."

I thanked Marcie and left. Mechanically, I walked to the car, opened the door, and sat inside. The rain had stopped, the sun had come out, and the air was stifling with the windows closed. Still I sat, silent, and stared at the dashboard.

It had to be a mistake.

Debra was alive. Debra was Liz. Therefore Liz was alive.

It was a basic syllogism. But it couldn't be true. There had to be some other explanation.

I thought of all the seemingly incontrovertible evidence that the feds had uncovered—more than enough to prosecute Bernie Wathen for murder. The airline tickets to St. Thomas, the ending of an affair, the phone call, the meeting, the fight, the blood, the fibers, the car—how could you explain the car, pulled from the bottom of that murky water? And what about Wathen's suicide? Surely not the action of an innocent man?

There had been only one flaw in the case: no body. Now I knew why.

Because that body was getting a haircut and dye job less than twenty miles away.

Chapter 20

I DON'T KNOW HOW LONG I sat in that parking lot. A few minutes, ten at the most, but a conviction was slowly forming. I knew, with same certainty that you know when someone loves you or the moment when they stop, that Liz had set up this whole thing.

The question was why.

The marriage had been unhappy. I got that. She had been involved in an affair, and it was ending. I got that, too. But why fake her own death? Why not just pack up and move away, get a divorce?

I already knew the answer. Because Liz had not just wanted to leave Pineyfield and Michael and Bernie behind. She had wanted to leave herself behind. She was looking for the ultimate fresh start, a true new beginning. It is something everyone fantasizes about now and then, sliding out of your own skin and waking up as someone else. To do it, though, must have taken months of planning. It wasn't just a knee jerk reaction to a break-up. Liz must have been thinking about this for a long time. Had the mood swings and the instability Michael witnessed been real symptoms of mental illness, or a part of a carefully orchestrated scene that could end convincingly with a suicide?

I thought about the phone call, and that is when I felt the first stirrings of anger. Liz had dredged me up from the past to add weight to the evidence of her instability. She knew I would arrive the next day, a friend so concerned about her emotional state that I would drive 300 miles to see her. If the police or her husband had any doubts about the accident or suicide, my story, added with her own recent behavior, would have been enough to quiet them.

None of this explained the forensic evidence found in the car. Bernie must have seen her that evening. He had offered no other alibi for the time of her death. Had she arranged to meet as a part of her plan or was it just happenstance? And why mention his name to me on the phone? Had she hoped only to hint at their affair, to expose him to gossip and ridicule, or had she wanted it to go further, to lead to a suspicion of murder?

Somewhere, Liz was now Debra Windler, free from an unhappy marriage, an unhappy affair, the bonds of motherhood, free—if the picture in the school had been accurate—even from her old body, her old face. She had been reborn. And Bernie Wathen was dead.

And I was the only person who knew the truth.

The situation was almost laughable. I, who had insisted that Wathen be made to pay, what was I supposed to do now? Go to the police on the heels of his suicide and says whoops, I made a mistake? Go to Michael, whose imprints might still be entwined with mine on the motel room sheets, and tell him that his wife was alive?

I thought I might throw up.

I realized then that the car windows were still up. I turned the key and opened them, then dropped my head to the steering wheel. I slowed my breathing and closed my eyes.

Before I did anything else, I had to be absolutely sure. I had to find Liz Bryson.

I went over the list of details in my head. I had no idea where she had gone. I had a description of Debra Windler, but no concrete proof that Liz and Windler were the same person, and besides, she could have changed her appearance a dozen times since she left this beachfront town. There was a social security number attached to Windler's name, so she could be tracked through anything attached to that—income, bank account, credit cards—but that kind of search would require hacking skills I did not possess. Perhaps the college information could be useful. And the Enterprise rent-a-car Marcie had mentioned would be something local.

I Googled rental agencies and found there was only one in town, on 87th street.

The Enterprise rental car sign stood beside a new garage, gas station, and car wash. I parked and rehearsed what I was going to say. As soon as I walked in the door, an older man wearing a blue work shirt with the name Ed stitched neatly in the front came out from the office.

"Are you the manager?" I asked loudly.

"Yes ma'am. Is there a problem?"

"Yes, there is definitely a problem. I have a condo down on Fortieth Street, and someone backed into and broke my planter. It was brand new last season, and I want something done about it!" I punctuated this last sentence by slapping the counter.

He seemed confused, which was exactly what I was going for.

"Ma'am, I'm sorry about your planter, but I can't see why—"

"It was one of your cars, that's why. Enterprise license plates. The neighbors told me. They were down for the week. Now that planter wasn't cheap—more than a hundred dollars—and it needs to be replaced."

Ed seemed to be making sense of this now, and he was getting a pencil and some kind of form on a large, legal-sized pad.

"What was the license number of the vehicle, ma'am?"

"How should I know?" I snapped.

He put the pencil down. "Do you have a description?"

"I told you. It was one of your cars."

He sighed. "Ma'am, I appreciate your problem. Really I do. But I need more than that to even look up the rental information to check on the, uh, accident. So if that's all you have…"

"Did I say that was all? The woman introduced herself to one of the neighbors that morning. Said her name was Debra something. Began with a 'W'."

This seemed to energize Ed a bit. He got out a large file box and began leafing through.

"How long ago would you say?"

"Early March, I think."

He looked for a few more minutes, then nodded. "Right here. Debra Windler. Hmmm, the address is local. 134th street. I can give her a call and ask her to fill out an accident report. The insurance won't pay without her statement."

I nodded, and he picked up the phone. A few minutes went by and he shook his head.

"It was a cell phone. Not in service."

I heard him dial information and see if there was a landline for the 134th street address. He hung up, disgusted.

"The address is one of those postal box places. I'll tell you, ma'am, you might need to file a police report. I don't really know how else we'll get in touch with her."

I sighed in mock frustration. "Can I get a copy of the rental agreement to take with me? The police might want that."

He looked it over a minute, then nodded. "She paid cash, so there's no credit card number. They might need her driver's license number, and that's on here. Hang on, I'll make you a copy."

Ed went into the cubicle and I heard the hum of an old Xerox machine. He came back with a fuzzy but legible copy and handed it to me.

"I hope this helps. The police get a statement from her, then we can file a claim."

"Thank you," I said, folding the paper carefully.

I was nearly to the door when he stopped me.

"Ma'am, what did you say your name was again?"

I smiled politely. "Marple. Jane Marple," I lied.

I turned and walked out of the door, hoping he was not an Agatha Christie buff. It was a relatively safe bet, but you never know.

Once in the car, I congratulated myself on my success. While Liz/Debra may have already applied for a license in another state, she would have had to use the previous license number as proof of identification. This, at least, was a start.

Chapter 21

I DROVE HOME TO IRVINGTON with Liz's boxes still firmly ensconced in the back of the car. I had gone through the first box haphazardly, and now I thought perhaps there could be more surprises inside. I wanted the time to comb through each and every piece of paper. I also wanted to talk to Wayne Kremm.

When I hit the Bay Bridge Tunnel it was late afternoon and the traffic on 64 on the Virginia side was already unbearable. I am always in awe of the people who travel in these mechanized herds each day, at their willingness to creep along or wait interminably for a light to change as the minutes of their lives tick inexorably by. I did not always view life this way, but I have seen its end come without warning, and I personally would not want to add a thousand hours in traffic to my own list of life's regrets.

I knew Wayne would probably be at his desk another hour or more. He seldom left work before six for anything except a clandestine interview or a tryst with a Congressman's wife. I normally avoid talking on the phone and driving at the same time, since I have never quite mastered my car's Bluetooth connection, but I didn't think it likely that I would lose control of my vehicle in the five m.p.h. back-up north of Norfolk. He picked up on the first ring, leading me to believe that it was a slow news day.

"Kremm."

"Wayne, it's Sandi."

His voice warmed considerably. "I knew you'd re-think my offer. Where do you want to meet?"

"Way outside of the District. Do you know La Grotta?"

I think he actually dropped the phone in his surprise. There was some significant fumbling and then he was back. "In Richmond? Is this a joke?"

"No, it's dinner. Or do you have other plans?"

"Be still my heart. Not that I want to look a gift horse in the mouth, to use a hackneyed phrase, but..."

I laughed. "It's just dinner, Wayne. I'm not inviting you to fly to Bermuda."

"Which would seem perfectly ordinary, except that I've asked you to dinner at least a dozen times in the past two years, and always with the same response. I'm not complaining, mind," he added, "I just want to know why my luck has changed, and why we're going to Richmond."

"Because I am in Norfolk now, and Richmond is closer for you."

"That answered one question."

I relented. "Look, Wayne, I need your help with something. That's it. I promise not to seduce you."

Wayne sighed with mock heaviness. "I suspected as much. Nothing's happening here anyway. What time?"

"How about seven? I'm about sixty miles south, but it could be two hours before I get there. I'll meet you in the bar."

"Sounds good. On my way."

I clicked off the cell and felt the slightest sense of relief. I had been keyed up since I discovered that Liz was almost certainly still alive, and the whole story played itself over and over in my head. I needed a third party, someone to listen and make suggestions, someone who would know what I could do with the handful of loose threads I held. I knew they led to Liz, but I didn't know how to follow them.

I made it to the restaurant in about ninety minutes, which wasn't bad, considering. It is a walk-down with a kind of wine cellar feel, crowded on weekends but nearly empty on a Monday night. A dozen or so customers (mostly couples) were talking quietly. I asked for a table for two and motioned to the most secluded one I could find. Then I ordered a Chianti and headed to the ladies room to survey the damage.

No one looks good after seven hours in a car, especially with the windows open. . My face was sallow, my hair flat, and all of my clothes were wrinkled. I washed my face and wetted down my hair in the sink, then crouched down to dry it under one of the hand dryers. This is a great trick if you have short hair—five minutes and it looks like you actually cared about your appearance—but it is a little awkward when other customers come in. A tall blonde with a long pony-tail stared at me pointedly as if I were some new species of homeless person. I smiled apologetically, but she didn't look appeased. After she left I applied more than the usual amount of blush, mascara, and even lip gloss. I didn't even try to deceive myself as to motive. I needed Wayne's help, and Wayne was much more helpful if physical attraction played a part.

Wayne got there just as the waiter brought my drink, and he ordered a dry martini. I raised my eyebrows.

"What? I can't drink martinis?"

"Is this a James Bond thing?" I asked jokingly.

He cast me a baleful look, as if he suspected me of taunting him. Wayne is not unattractive, but he is a far cry from the film version of a secret agent. Wayne is no more than five feet, four inches with his shoes on, and while he is solidly built, he gives the impression of heaviness. He does have thick, curly brown hair and an impish smile, but he also has deep lines around his eyes from perpetually squinting at the computer and a nose that could chisel granite. A romantic might say that his was a face with personality, a lived-in face, but he always reminded me of something out of Tolkien.

"If you're going to insult me..." he warned.

"I wouldn't dream of it. Honestly. Sit down and relax."

The waiter returned with his martini, which Wayne eyed with suspicion.

"No one can make a good martini in less than two minutes," he said, shaking his head.

"Have two and you won't notice," I suggested.

Wayne sipped his drink, then peered at me closely.

"What happened to you? I haven't seen you this wound up in... come to think of it, I've never seen you this wound up. Did you win the lottery? Publish a book? Fall in love?"

I blushed unintentionally at the last, but I shook my head when he chortled, "Ah ha!"

"No 'ah ha'," I corrected. "I have become involved in another mystery, and I need some advice."

"But there is a man involved," he persisted.

I nodded reluctantly. "Yes, but that is actually part of the problem. Now, do you want to stop talking so I can tell you, or do you want to badger me all night?"

"Badgering sounds exciting," he answered with a twinkle.

"Enough. Do you remember the story I gave you about the woman in

Pineyfield?"

"Of course. Great story. I even did a follow-up after the guy—what was his name? Wathen?—after he did himself in. Why? Oh," he said, realization sinking in, "he didn't do it?"

The revelations of the day had made me edgy and short-tempered. I pushed my chair back from the table in frustration.

"Jesus, Wayne, would you just listen for five minutes and stop jumping to conclusions?"

"Sorry," he said, surprised and somewhat chastened. "Occupational hazard."

I explained about the boxes, the mailbox, and the hairdresser. When I got to the date and time that Debra/Liz had been getting her cut and color, he spilled his martini.

"You're telling me she wasn't in the car?"

I nodded.

"That's... wow. That's amazing. Okay, so if she didn't die—"

"Then Bernie Wathen wasn't a murderer, and I helped kill an innocent man."

"Wait a minute." Wayne shook his head vehemently. "Stop right there. You didn't do anything except tell the truth as far as you knew it. Believe me, Sandi, I've been there before. If Wathen hadn't lied about his relationship with Elizabeth Bryson, and if he had told everyone he was there at the time of the accident, it wouldn't have gone down that way. That was his choice, not yours. Right? The question here is, did she just want an out, or was she looking to take her ex-lover down at the same time?"

"I don't know. There are so many what-if's and why's and how's, you know? So many questions. Like, why was there her blood in the car if he didn't kill her? How did she get the car off the bridge without going over herself? How did she get away without being seen? Where the hell is she now?" I ran my hands through my short, blonde hair. "It's enough to drive you crazy."

Wayne looked at me thoughtfully. "All along I've been thinking of your friend as a victim. Let's try it another way. She's sick of her marriage and her life. She knows that a divorce will mean shared custody, splitting assets, being trapped in an apartment with three kids until she's too old to play the field." I made a snorting noise at this, but he held up his hand. "I know, older women are beautiful. I've heard it. But think like her for a minute. She wants to walk away, really away. Reinvent herself. So she's smart, right? Maybe even brilliant. She finds this girl who died who would have been a little younger than she is. She gets a social security card, gets some little low-credit-line cards, then a driver's license. She starts to change her own appearance, but slowly—loses weight but still wears baggy clothes, maybe even starts to let herself go a little in public."

"I've already thought of all that. But what about Bernie? And why call me?"

"Stay with me here," Wayne said, and his eyes gleamed with excitement. "The affair is real. I mean, she has it, for whatever reason. Maybe she figures she'll leave him along with everything else, but then he rejects her. She gets pissed, thinks, fine, when I go, I'm going to make sure everybody knows about us. She'd know how much that would hurt him in that community. So she starts to act wigged out, calls you, suggests that Bernie's involved and—wham. She disappears, you're bound to say something, and she figures that will be enough to start the rumors and ruin him."

This was exactly what I had been thinking when I left the hairdresser's that morning, but the confirmation felt like steel bands tightening around my chest. The pain of betrayal was almost physical, almost palpable. Still, something was off, out of focus. I knew what it was, but I wanted him to discount it, to dismiss it as chimerical.

"Why would she want to meet Bernie that night? The affair would have become public knowledge without it. It really made it more dangerous for her, not less. And she had to know his brother would cover for him, so it might not have even come out that he was there."

The waiter came back and Wayne pointed to our glasses, then hurried him off with a wave of his hand.

"Unless... unless she didn't want it to look like a suicide."

"But then why all of the psychological hysterics beforehand? Liz set herself up to look like the perfect candidate for suicide," I noted.

"True. Maybe that was her plan, but then she thinks, hey, why leave that on my husband, my kids, when I can blame it on this asshole instead? Suppose she plants evidence in her car, gets him there hoping there will be an eyewitness and calls you for a little extra insurance?"

I disagreed, playing the devil's advocate. "How could she know I would get that involved? I could just as easily have changed my mind and called the next day and then not even gone to the funeral."

Wayne's face softened and he smiled slightly. "Sandi, think about it. She knew you were lonely—"

"I'm alone, not lonely. There's a difference," I argued.

"Fine, alone. If she has kept up with you at all on Facebook, she knows you're a sucker for a sob story. You are, you know it, so don't argue," he said before I could retort. "She also would have known that death, any death, would bring back what happened with Ryan. Suppose she was counting on that, counting on you pouring all the energy that you couldn't use after Ryan's accident into looking for answers here?"

"You're saying Liz chose me to frame Bernie Wathen for her murder, and I didn't even know it?" I felt cold.

"I don't know," Wayne said, shaking his head as if to clear it. "It's a stretch, but then, so is Liz walking around somewhere as Debra Windler. And you've got to remember, you didn't frame him. All you did was ask the logical questions, but they were questions only an outsider would ask. When everyone scrambled to cover it, they looked guilty. "

Our second round was delivered to our table, and Wayne ordered us both dinner without asking me. I felt dizzy.

"San, don't take it personally," Wayne said.

"Don't take it personally? How can I not take it personally? She used me," I said, voice rising.

"People use me all the time. One politician leaks something that gives him an advantage. So his opponent gives me a tip that will ruin the guy. I do all the footwork, I print it, but later the story goes sour. That's life," Wayne said.

"It's not my life," I retorted.

"You want answers, right? The only way to do that is to go to the source. Ask her. Isn't that what you want to do?"

I nodded.

"So what do we have?"

I hadn't told him about the driver's license number. When I did, he laughed aloud.

"Come work for me! I'll pay you whatever you want. I can hardly believe you haven't been doing this all your life."

"The problem is, I haven't been doing this all of my life, and I don't have a clue how to take this any further. "

"Ah, so now we come to why you agreed to my questionably charming company at dinner. We need someone to run the license for a new address. Believe it or not, all of the states have not yet networked their DMV records, but if she's on the East Coast or any major metropolitan area, she should come right up. I have a source in the state police. She won't be in now, but give me the number and I'll have her run it in the morning."

"Her?"

"Dare I hope you are jealous? No?" He grinned.

Our food came and we let the talk wander to other, lighter things, though we were both preoccupied. By the time the check came, Wayne had grown serious again.

"Sandi, is there something more to this? I mean, I understand why you would want to know what happened, but I get the feeling that isn't everything."

I looked at him, and I suppose the answer was written all over my face.

"Oh, shit. It's her husband, isn't it? You've gotten involved with her husband."

I hastened to explain. "We're not really involved. It was just one time, and I don't even know if it is going anywhere."

He looked at me pityingly. "Of course it's going to go somewhere. It already has. This is the first guy since Ryan died, isn't it? No—don't give me that look. I'm just saying—you don't do meaningless relationships. I'm proof of that."

I didn't say anything. There was no point.

"All right, I understand why you want to find her. I'd feel the same way if it were me. But this could be a little hairier than you think."

"What do you mean? I thought you said your friend could run the number."

"Finding her isn't the part that worries me. Think about it a minute, Sandi. I'm sure she has been keeping up on the investigation. It apparently didn't bother her conscience to see Wathen arrested for her murder. If you approach her, I don't know how far she'd go to stay hidden."

"Are you saying she'd hurt me? Don't you think that's a little far-fetched?" I protested. "After all, we were friends."

"Yeah, and Wathen was her lover."

I hadn't looked at it quite that way.

"Okay. Point taken."

Wayne picked up the check over my protests and walked me to my car.

"Another thing," he said as I unlocked the door. "Since you've gotten involved with the husband, you might want to let me look into it instead."

"I don't see—"

"Don't get all defensive on me. All I'm saying is, it's a conflict of interest. If you have proof that she faked her own death, then crimes have been committed. Not just setting up Wathen, but insurance fraud, stealing identities, falsifying documents... If the time comes, knowing what it would do to her husband and her children, could you turn her in?"

I shrugged, defeated and exhausted. "I don't know."

"Then hand it off to me."

I had a sudden thought and looked at him in alarm. "Wayne, I trusted you! You wouldn't print this!"

"You know me well enough to know that I wouldn't bring it out unless you wanted me to. I just mean that I'm willing to take it if you can't, and if ends up getting dangerous, well, it might be useful to let her know that you aren't the only one who is on her trail. Okay?" He was trying to be protective, and it was endearing.

"Okay."

He gave me a last grin as I got in my car. "You sure you don't want me to come home with you?"

"You're incorrigible," I laughed.

The drive home was nearly two hours, mostly on darkened backroads. I tuned the radio to a country station and imagined my mind as a huge chalkboard, then slowly wiped it clean. I concentrated on the road, the white and yellow lines slipping beneath the tires, the quiet hum beneath my seat. There would be time enough to think in the morning.

Chapter 22

I SPENT THE NEXT FEW days attending to the mundane details of life. I wrote checks, did the necessary cleaning and upkeep on the boat, met with two new clients and got a baseball card collection back for a guy whose wife had thrown him out of the house. I gave my evenings to combing through the file folders and scouring the Internet for any signs of Debra Windler. There was nothing, no other scrap of paper, no random bits of data, to provide any clue as to her whereabouts.

And Michael didn't call.

I stared at the phone a half-dozen times a night, wishing it would ring, wanting to hear his voice. At the same time, I was relieved he didn't. He believed his wife had been murdered, and this had released him from the guilt of an unhappy marriage and his own inadequate efforts as a husband that followed the initial suspicions of suicide. If he knew that instead she had planned—for months, perhaps years—to leave their life behind, what would it do to him? His children could grow up with the regret for her loss far more easily than the shame of her abandonment. How could I tell him? And how could I talk to him if everything I said was a lie?

I found myself half-hoping that, like me, Wayne would find no trace of Debra Windler. In the meantime, I made a bargain with myself that, even if Michael called, I would remain silent about Liz until I knew something more. If she couldn't be found, then wasn't she as good as dead?

It had been four days since my dinner with Wayne, and I still hadn't heard anything when Michael called.

It was late evening, but the air was summer hot now. There is often no real spring in tidewater Virginia. It is cold, it rains until you think you will scream, and then, after perhaps a handful of bright, clear days, the temperature climbs to ninety and the humidity hovers at eighty percent. Most of the liveaboards take this opportunity to head north and cruise the New England coast, but I don't mind the heat. There is a private yacht club next to the marina, and the dockmaster there lets me swim laps in the pool after closing on nights when the clubhouse is empty. I swim until my chest and shoulders ache, loving the sensation of the cold liquid slipping over and around me. I had been doing this, swimming until I could barely see the pool walls in the faint twilight, and had just finished toweling off on the deck when the cell rang. I still had on my damp bathing suit, so I sat on cockpit floor to avoid putting wet spots on the cushions. Nothing ever dried in the summer here. If you spilled water on the rug in June, you could count on it still being moist in August.

"Hello?" I said, settling my back against the pedestal.

"San? It's Michael."

He sounded a little hesitant, and I wondered if he thought he should have called me before now, or if he wasn't sure he should be calling at all.

"Hi, Michael. How's everything going?" I achieved a friendly but cautious tone.

"Good, I guess. The realtor called tonight. She's got a couple who want the house, and they pre-qualified for a V.A. loan, so it should be quick. She thinks we might be able to settle inside of a week," he said.

"That's really fast. Wow."

"Yeah, even the realtor was impressed. I won't make much off of the sale, but we don't really need it."

He seemed to want to say something else, but he stopped and we had a few seconds of dead space.

"So, how's your job going? How are the kids?"

Michael sounded relieved to have the conversation continued, and he warmed to this topic immediately. "The kids are doing really well. Lizzie's in preschool and my mom is keeping the other two during the day. They really seem happy here. As for the job, well, it's okay. I can't say it is really exciting, and their biggest financial operation is making sure everyone gets their paychecks, but the money isn't bad and they are letting me flex my hours around the kids."

"That sounds great."

The conversation fell dead again. The burden of what I knew was pushing at the front of my brain so much I was afraid I might blurt out the whole seamy story involuntarily with my next breath.

Michael cleared his throat.

"I, uh, I've missed you. I've been thinking about you, and what happened at the beach." His voice drifted off, lost.

"I've been thinking about you, too."

At least this was not a lie. Despite my best efforts, it was often all I thought about.

"We have a big family reunion here in August, and I was wondering if maybe, you know, you might want to come back here to visit."

My mouth felt dry. A family reunion was the place widowers brought prospective replacements to be evaluated by the powers that be—which would be great except I knew Michael was no widower.

"Um, I have a conference in August, but maybe we can work it out," I answered.

There was another pause as I imagined him trying to categorize my response as positive or negative.

"Look, I'm not trying to push you into anything," Michael said, letting out a long sigh. "I know we said that we were going to take this whole thing pretty slowly, but the thing is, I really do care about you. I mean, I think we could really, you know, work out. Like I said before. The timing isn't the best, but I'm kind of afraid to just let it go. Do you know what I mean?"

My body tingled and my head was buzzing the way it does when you stand up quickly and think you might faint. I rested my cheek against the cool, smooth fiberglass of the pedestal and closed my eyes.

"Yes. I know what you mean."

"So I want to see you, to be with you. Can we do that?" he asked.

"I'm not sure I'm ready to meet your family, Michael," I said carefully. "I think we need to spend more than one weekend together before we show up as a couple in front of your children. I don't want to upset anyone, and I don't want to disappoint them, either. Do you understand?"

"Then let's spend time together. I'll try to schedule the settlement for next Friday morning and leave the kids with my parents. I could be in Virginia by Friday afternoon."

"You do know that I live on a boat," I warned.

Michael laughed, and I was reminded of how it lit up his face.

"I think I can handle it. Can you handle me for the weekend?"

"Sure."

"I'll let you know as soon as the date is set. Is everything else going okay for you?"

"Sure," I lied. "Same old same old."

"I'll give you a call sometime next week. Okay?"

"Okay."

"Night, San."

"Goodnight."

I hung up the phone. I was alternating between a kind of jubilant excitement—he likes me, he wants me—and the sense of impending doom that came from the weight of the secret I kept from him. Suppose I truly did love him? Could I carry this kind of secret through a marriage?

I shivered despite the warm air and went below to shower. I poured a glass of pinot and carried it into the shower with me, then turned the water to scald. The hot steam of the tiny bathroom soothed me and eased the tension that built in my neck and shoulders as we had talked. By the time I finished and wrapped myself in an oversized white terry robe, I managed to convince myself that I really had no choice but to keep the existence of Debra Windler from Michael for his own sake and the sake of his children.

I got my laptop and was just settling down to write an email for a client when the phone rang. It was Wayne.

"I'm sorry I didn't get back to you before this. My police friend called today," Wayne said, his voice sounding tired.

"Well?"

"Nothing. She hasn't applied for a new license anywhere, or if she has, it isn't as Debra Windler. We've got nothing."

I breathed a sigh that was both disappointment and relief.

"So what do you think we should do from here?"

There was a pause and I could feel Wayne thinking.

"It depends on what you want, San. Look, you could turn this whole thing over to the cops or the Feds and they'd find her. But that would take any control you have right out of the equation. You could keep looking for her yourself, but it's gonna be tough from here. I already ran an Internet search, and I got nothing there. If you had a social, maybe you could find somebody to run it and see if she's working anywhere. And you do have the bank statement and the credit card statement. Either one might come up with a new address, but you're going to have a hell of a time getting anyone to give it to you. Or, third choice, you could just forget about it."

"I wish I could," I said with a sigh.

"Yeah, I know. Believe me, I wish I didn't know half the stuff I've learned in this job. But sometimes you just have to close the door on something, walk away," he said. "Heard from the husband—what's his name, Michael?"

"Yes. He is planning on coming to see me this weekend. He wants me to go to a family reunion in August."

Wayne whistled. "Sounds serious. Look, my advice to you is, just let it go."

"I want to. I do. But I don't know if I can. It's not like she can come back, anyway. But if I knew she were settled somewhere, happy…"

"There are no guarantees, San. Even if she is living the good life as Debra Windler, she could end up as the victim of a crime, they could run her DNA, and Liz Bryson's name would pop up. You end up with this guy, and that will always be there, in the back of your mind."

It hadn't been in my mind at all until he said it.

"Thanks for that. Like I don't have enough to worry about," I said.

"I'm sorry. Occupational hazard—I always choose the most lurid story line," Wayne said cheerfully. "Look, chances are you will never see or hear from her or about her again. But before, when we were in Richmond, you said you felt like you had to know."

"If you couldn't find her, it doesn't matter."

"You've still got the bank and credit card stuff. You could try that."

I shook my head, though he couldn't see it.

"I don't know, Wayne. I need to think about it."

"Sure. If it were me, I'd start with the bank. Maybe say she has a rent deposit coming back or something, and she listed her account through them on her application. Try the same thing with the credit card company. Chances are they'll shut you down, but you might get lucky."

"Okay. Thanks, Wayne. I really appreciate everything you've done."

"I haven't done much. But if you decide you aren't really interested in this Bryson guy, you know I would be happy to be your rebound date," he said lightly.

I laughed. "You really don't give up, do you?"

"Never. Take care, San. Keep me updated if you get anything."

"You'll be the first person I call. Good night, Wayne."

"Night."

I sat a long time, staring at the cell phone.

I knew I should try to do what was right… but right for whom?

So what I did was nothing at all.

Chapter 23

MICHAEL ARRIVED FRIDAY AFTERNOON.

It was one of those mild and pleasant June days, with a brilliant blue sky that could have been October and a warm southwesterly breeze. I had ditched all of the many tasks I should have accomplished and had instead taken the boat out for a sail. The wind blew a steady fifteen knots and I carved a straight line of white foam on blue water across the bay and back. It was the sort of day when you set the sails and let go of the wheel, and she balances perfectly; you can finger-fine-tune the slightest adjustments, and then lean back against the lifelines and watch her fly.

I came back in around midday. The sun was warm and the breeze had started to die off. I dropped the main and tacked almost to the dock on the jib. As I started the engine and rolled it in, I saw a tall, lean figure on the dock. I recognized him even with the sunlight in my eyes. I shouted and waved. He grabbed the dock lines and came forward as I pulled slowly into the slip.

I ran forward and grabbed the line he tossed me.

"Hey," I said, but I couldn't keep the sheer joy from my face.

"Hey."

He smiled at me, and I was struck breathless by the warmth of his eyes.

In the time since I had last seen Michael, he seemed to have grown healthier. His hair was shorter and fell in smooth waves about his face. His shoulders seemed broader and his stomach flatter. Of course, there is much to the old adage that absence makes the heart grow fonder.

I secured the lines and climbed off. When I put my foot on the dock, he came forward and took me in his arms. It felt like home.

I nestled into his chest and closed my eyes. He kissed my hair. In a perfect world, it was a moment that shouldn't end. But this wasn't a perfect world.

"So," I said, stepping back and breaking away. "Welcome to the Northern Neck."

He looked surprised at my sudden withdrawal. "Thanks."

"You missed a great sail," I said quickly, busying myself with lines. "Tomorrow's supposed to be windy, too. We can go out then. Or we can anchor out somewhere tonight. Whatever you want."

"San," Michael said softly, taking my arm.

I tried to look away, but his eyes caught and held me.

"I came down here to be with you. Okay?"

I nodded mutely.

"So whatever you want to do, that's fine with me. And if you don't want to do anything, that's okay, too. Now," he smiled but toughened his voice, "I just drove about six hours and I need a drink."

I smiled, feeling relieved. I would let him take control of the weekend. How hard was that? I would put everything on auto-pilot and let him chart a course and figure how much distance to cover. As for Liz—for these few days at least, she could stay at the bottom of Assateague bay.

"Beer or wine?"

"Beer. I can't handle wine in the middle of the day."

"Come on aboard then."

Michael climbed over the lifelines with his duffle bag and followed me below. It had been a long time since I'd had a guest aboard (those two F.B.I. guys didn't really count as guests, and I don't think they even let themselves realize they were on a boat), and I felt uncomfortably like I was seeing it all for the first time through someone else's eyes.

We had worked hard on this boat, Ryan and I. It was an older sloop, thirty-eight feet in length, and neglected by its previous owner. We had brought it back to life, polishing brass and varnishing each board in the teak and holly sole until it shone. Since I had moved aboard full-time, I had added a Berber rug and throw pillows and filled the shelves with books. Unfortunately, I had not noticed until this minute the vague shadowy rectangular stains on the walls where I had taken down the pictures of Ryan and me. The boat had once been a testament to our relationship, and I had somehow thought that removing those photos would dull the power of my memories. The marks on the wall were proof that I was depressingly unsuccessful.

Michael, however, did not seem to notice. "Wow. This is great."

"Thanks. Do you want the grand tour?"

"Absolutely."

I showed him the tiny head and took him forward to the small stateroom with a V-berth. It was the bed I slept in in the days following Ryan's death, clinging to an old shirt of his so I could still have the scent of him before I slept. Now, having Michael here, I wondered if this had been a mistake. We could have gone away, gone to a hotel, and avoided facing the benevolent ghost that inhabited this ship.

I must have stood motionless in front of the bed for a minute or more before Michael touched my arm.

"Thank you for bringing me here," he said.

I turned to him, and he took me in his arms and kissed me.

We kissed long and deep, and then he lowered me to the bed. He undressed me gently, and we made love like two virgins in the soft white light. I had never touched skin like his, he had never touched skin like mine... we were like explorers in some unknown country, feeling our way. The movement of our bodies seemed as essential as breath. Each moment was complete, a perfect sphere, unending, and yet leading to the next so that the whole afternoon slipped by like pearls on a string. We must have both fallen asleep, and when I opened my eyes again it was twilight. Michael was awake and had been watching my face.

"You're beautiful."

"I'm glad you think so."

"I don't have to think at all. You just are."

He kissed my forehead.

"So, now what?"

I stretched and yawned. All of the awkwardness and discomfort of the day had vanished as if it had never been.

"Dinner," I said definitively.

We got up, showered, dressed, and went to a local seafood restaurant for dinner. We talked about the children, our jobs, places we'd love to see. After we finished dinner and drank a bottle of wine, we went back to the boat and made love again.

That night I dreamed I was out sailing in a storm, and Ryan was with me. Suddenly, in the way of dreams, I was on a ride in an amusement park, laughing, but it wasn't Ryan next to me at all, it was Michael. And then I was in a kind of cave like a haunted house, riding in a small open boat, only

I got off the ride and started walking through the dark display. I looked down in a small pool of water and saw Liz's face, white and bloated with her hair long and dark and floating. I screamed, and she opened her eyes and smiled. I woke up with a jolt.

It was still dark and my body was wet with sweat.

Chapter 24

MICHAEL STAYED FOR SATURDAY AND Sunday. I admit now that I justified our time together as something we both needed and deserved and for those two days, at least waking, I was able to forget about Liz. Yes as soon as I closed my eyes each night, a variation of the same dream disturbed my sleep. It is ironic, really. I was haunted by two ghosts, one a man I have loved and lost and the other a woman who was not even dead. Yet Michael was untroubled, and so I buried my own doubts and fears beneath the impossible hope that we could somehow stop time and live forever in this moment.

It wasn't until Sunday night that Michael broached the subject of our future. We were lying in the front V-berth, watching a movie. He had the remote and turned the sound low.

"So," he said.

"So?" I had a sense of what was coming, and I tried mentally to ward it off to no avail.

"Do you think you could live in West Virginia?"

The way he had phrased it gave me an out, I thought.

"I don't know. Could you live in Virginia?"

He frowned.

"I don't have a job here, and really, neither do you," he pointed out. "I have family there. You are flexible, and what you do, you could do anywhere. So it seems like West Virginia would make the most sense."

I felt myself bristling at his tone.

"There isn't a lot of open water in West Virginia," I pointed out.

"A boat isn't a life," Michael answered.

But of course, it had been. And even if he was right, who was he to say so?

"It is to me," I retorted.

He sighed, turned away from me slightly, and turned up the sound.

I think it was the secret I kept that made me react as I did. He had no idea what I had been going through, or how unlikely it was that our relationship had a future. I reached for the remote and turned off the movie. Then I sat up, crossed-legged, on the bed.

"Don't ever do that."

"Do what?" He actually looked surprised.

"Shut me down. Don't do it. I don't care if that's how you've handled your problems in the past, that's not how I do it."

Michael looked at me silently for several minutes. I waited him out.

"All right," he said finally. "Then let's talk about it. Suppose I want you to move back to West Virginia, marry me, and be a mother to my kids. You would rather live alone on this boat. How is that supposed to make me feel?"

It was my turn to be surprised. "Marry you? Michael, we have had—what? Fifty or sixty hours together at the most? And I am supposed to give up my business, my home, and my independence, to move to West Virginia? And as for being a mother, I have barely met your children. I'm not ready for that, and neither are they. I have no idea how to be a mother."

"Believe me, you couldn't do any worse than Liz did. They don't know what a real mother is," he said, then held up his hands as if to ward off any remarks I might make in defense of Liz, not knowing how little there was to defend.

I took a deep breath. This was going nowhere.

"Look, Michael, let's just let it be for now. It's too soon to make any kind of commitments. I don't want to end up feeling trapped and hating you six months from now." It was my turn to hold up my hands as he raised himself on an elbow, face reddening. "I don't want you to feel trapped and stuck with me, either."

His jaw was tight, and he looked away.

"Look, let's just enjoy this for a while," I said reaching for his hand. "Okay?"

He sighed. "You're right. I guess... I'm lonely. I've been lonely for a long time. I need someone in my life. The kids need someone. That doesn't mean," he added quickly," that I was looking for the first person to come along. I care about you. I thought this would be good for both of us."

"I understand," I said, squeezing his hand. "Why don't we just agree to take it slowly?"

He nodded.

"All right. But I want to bring the kids down with me next time."

I froze.

"If you think they are ready for that."

"I do. Not to stay on the boat," he hastened to add. "We can stay at the hotel. But this way you could spend some time with the kids and they'd feel like they had a little vacation."

"I don't know," I said hesitantly. "Lizzie would be fine, but I don't know about the other two."

"Joshua is two-and-a-half, and he loves the water. He'd think the pool was great. As for Katie, I think I might leave her here with Mom. She won't know the difference, and it will give me a chance to focus on the other two."

I didn't know how to tell him that I found the thought of two children to be nothing short of petrifying. It's not that I don't like children, but my experience with them is severely limited. I had wanted to have children with Ryan, but I had always pictured our children as somehow different than the snotty-nosed, unwashed hordes I saw in the local Walmart. I had only seen Michael's children briefly, but little Lizzie looked like an emotional time bomb and the toddler was definitely high maintenance. Perhaps I would not measure up to Michael's concept of motherhood, fall short as Liz had fallen short. Or, if I were honest, perhaps I realized that I could love them, that they could easily become everything to me, and then they could be stripped from me.

"San?"

The pause lengthened to a formidable silence. I shook myself both mentally and physically.

"No, it sounds great. Really."

And when I said it, it really did.

We agreed on the following weekend, and that closed the discussion. In the back of my mind I felt all of the pricks of conscience for what I had held back from him, but I was able to push them away. We made love tenderly then, without urgency or passion. When it was over, Michael immediately fell asleep, and I lay awake for hours after, listening to the sound of his breathing.

I don't know when I finally fell asleep, but it was just before daylight when I woke. Michael needed to leave by six, and he was already up and dressing. I looked out of the porthole and saw that the sky hung heavy and dark over the water.

"Looks like rain," I said.

"Yeah, I noticed. It will slow down traffic, so I need to get going."

Perhaps it was the coming storm, but I could not shake an ominous feeling as I walked him to his car. It seemed to permeate the air, and even to taint his kiss goodbye.

"What is it?" Michael asked, stepping back from me but still holding my hand.

"What do you mean?"

"I feel like there's something you're not saying, something you don't want to tell me."

I held my breath. I was afraid the words would burst from my lips of their own accord.

"I know, I'm being paranoid, right?" he said, shaking his head. "I'm sorry. I guess I just don't want to leave you. I'll call you tonight, okay?"

"Okay. Drive safe."

I stood still in the parking lot as I watched him pull away.

Chapter 25

BY EIGHT O'CLOCK THAT MORNING, I made the decision.

I would make one more attempt to locate Debra Windler.

If I failed, maybe the dreams would stop. Maybe I would be able to look Michael in the face without reservation. Maybe I could see a way forward for both of us.

If I succeeded… well, then I would have another decision to make.

As I stood under the soothing water of the shower I mentally rehearsed what to say when I called the bank. I tried and rejected a variety of approaches. As I was rinsing the conditioner from my hair I remembered I also had the letter from that college. Many colleges still use a social security number as a student I.D. number, so they might have it on her transcript. I could find a way to request a copy and see.

After dressing I went through the files that I had again and laid out the bank and credit card statements and the college letter. I placed my first call to the First National Bank of Delaware, Rehoboth Beach office. A woman answered.

"Hi, this is Sandra Beck." I decided to use my own name at this point. The best lies have an element of the truth, and besides, I was afraid I couldn't keep all the aliases straight. "I am trying to contact one of your customers, but she moved and has not left a forwarding address at the post office."

"One moment, please. I'll transfer you to the manager," the voice said efficiently.

While the recorded music played, I groused to myself. I had hoped to get someone less official who might not know the ethics involved in providing customer information. That obviously hadn't worked out.

"Rodney Coffman. How may I help you?" A deep voice that sounded out of breath snapped me from my reverie.

"Hi, Mr. Coffman. My name is Sandra Beck," I said in what I hoped was a firm and professional tone. "I rented an apartment to a customer of yours last year and she recently moved. I mailed out the refund of her deposit to her box number, but it came back with a stamp that said there was no forwarding address. I know from her application that her account was with your bank, and I was wondering if you had an address or number where she could be reached."

"Well, Ms. Beck, we do not normally give out personal customer information without prior approval, but if you hold on a moment, I'll see what we can do." There was a sound of a chair moving and typing on a keyboard. "Now, what was your renter's name?"

I told him. He breathed heavily into the phone for few minutes, and I got the impression of a huge man straining over a ponderous belly to reach the keys.

"Windler. She closed her account with us in March through our website, no forwarding address given."

"So you have no idea where she might be now," I said.

"No, although..."More key punching and heavy breathing. "I'd guess not local. She emptied out her account over a couple of days at an ATM in Atlanta."

"Atlanta, Georgia?" I repeated, feeling a sense of excitement.

"Yes. Of course, that doesn't mean she's still there. I'd say you just need to hold the deposit in escrow and if she doesn't come to claim it, well, that's her loss."

I agreed that this seemed like the best idea and thanked him for his trouble. He sounded as if the effort had nearly killed him, but he wheezed graciously and assured me it had been no problem at all. I extricated myself from the conversation as politely as possible, and it was all I could do not to cheer when I finally got off the phone. I knew something! I had a city and a state. It was true that she might have been passing through, but I had a gut feeling, an instinct, that she was still there.

My next call was to La Vrae University. I asked the switchboard operator for records. A young voice picked up.

"Records."

"Hi. I'd like to get a copy of my transcripts if I could?"

"Sure. Name?"

"Debra Windler."

There was a brief pause and the voice returned.

"You have already used your complimentary copy, so there will be a charge of four dollars. Do you want me to charge that to your credit card on record?"

"Sure," I said gratefully.

"Ms. Windler, would you also like me to use your Atlanta address?"

I paused, not daring to take a breath.

"Ms. Windler?"

My mind raced.

"You know, this is kind of embarrassing, but I've been living with a couple of different people in the last few months, and I don't remember what address you have," I said with a nervous laugh.

The voice sounded somewhat condescending. "I have you at 8117 Orangewood Court, Atlanta. Will that do?"

There was a decision here. If I said yes, I lost the social. If I said no, I would definitely arouse suspicion. I decided to take what I had and go with it.

"Yeah, that's it. Thanks."

"You should receive your transcript in three to five business days. Please contact us if we can be of further service," she said in a monotone which mimicked a computer voice. The phone clicked off before I could respond.

I scrambled for a pencil and wrote down the address. She was in Atlanta, and if she wanted transcripts, she had been looking for a job of a paralegal. Her savings had probably run out by now. It had been more than three months. There was a strong possibility that she had gotten a job, and that right now she sat at a desk in a law firm somewhere. I was definitely a step closer than I had been before.

I called information and asked for a number for Debra Windler at the address I had been given by La Vrae. I didn't really expect to find anything. After all of the precautions she had taken, I really couldn't see Liz having a landline and a listed number available to anyone who had found her name. Besides, it should have come up on Wayne's Internet search. I was not surprised when no number was listed.

My next step was to go to the laptop. I punched in the Atlanta address. In a few seconds, directions and a map loaded on to my laptop. The address was located in a suburban shopping mall. Even before I zoomed in, I knew—another mailbox-for-rent.

Frustrated, I slammed the lid of the laptop. Atlanta was what, a city of a few million people? I had less chance of finding her now than when I had started. I dialed Wayne's Post desk.

"You do love me," Wayne said facetiously when I identified myself.

I sighed. I was not in the mood to verbally joust. "Like a brother. I need to vent."

"So cold, so cruel." He sighed. "So, you decided to keep digging, didn't you? Is this bad news as in, 'I found her' or bad news as in 'I didn't find her'?"

"Neither," I said, and explained what I had learned. Wayne sounded more upbeat than I felt.

"You are clearly not a real investigative reporter. What do you think, the information falls in our laps? Research is ninety percent repetitive phone calls and ten percent discovery. Hey, that's not bad. I should have a poster made for my staff."

"I don't have a staff," I pointed out.

"True. I may be able to help you there. You do know what you need to do next."

I hated to admit ignorance, but I had no idea.

"Not a clue, Wayne."

"Aw, baby. You disappoint me," he said, with what I know was a self-satisfied smirk. "Look, you think she's a paralegal. There are probably no more than a few hundred law firms in the Atlanta area. So..."

"I call each one and ask for Debra Windler?"

"Bingo."

I let out a frustrated moan. "Wayne, even at three minutes a call, that's—"

"A lot of minutes. Good thing you have Uncle Wayne to help out."

"Uncle Wayne? Please."

"Don't mock. I have a dozen eager little summer interns from all the best colleges who will jump right on this. They won't have a clue what it's about," he added seriously. "If I told them to dance naked in the local car wash, they'd think they were supporting a run for a Pulitzer."

I laughed, that particular vision conjured up in my mind. "Oh, Wayne—I love you, but someday saying things like that will get you fired."

"So they say. Okay, we might not be able to get to it until the end of the week. I already have the little darlings running down some gun lobbyists. Any message you want them to give her if they find her?"

I thought a moment. "No. Hang up, lie, I don't know. I don't want her to know anyone is looking. Not yet."

I could feel him nodding in agreement. "Okay. I'll get back to you."

"Um, Wayne."

"Uh oh. The infamous 'Um, Wayne'."

"Michael is bringing the children down this Friday. I'm not... I still don't know what I'm going to tell him, or if I'm going to tell him anything at all. So even if you have something definite by then..."

He sounded sympathetic, an unusual tone for Wayne. "Yeah, I'll sit on it till next week."

"Thanks. I—"

"I know. You love me. So you said. Take care, San. Don't get in too deep," Wayne warned lightly.

"You know me. No problem."

I hung up the phone with a vague sense of disquiet. It was actually possible, even likely, that Wayne and his hordes of summer interns could find Liz. It was an understatement to say that this complicated my relationship with Michael. I would be auditioning for the role of mother next weekend, when their real mother was quite possibly alive and well in Atlanta, less than a thousand miles away.

Chapter 26

I HAD ONLY ONE CASE left to finish up that week. Summer is my slow time. Not that human nature becomes more forgiving and generous in the warm months, it just seems that people are more willing to let things go, or put them off until some unnamed date in the future. Perhaps it is only when the nights are long that people take the time to access the wrongs done to them and seek retribution. Instead I spent my time cleaning up the boat and trying to imagine everything two small children would like to eat and drink. My pantry, usually confined to cereal and pasta, was now overflowing with cookies and pudding and crackers of all shapes and sizes. I stocked the fridge with boxes of juice and kid-sized yogurt. I even went to the local Walmart and purchased a basket of pool toys—foam noodles, soft balls, floats with cartoon characters emblazoned on the sides. There was barely room in the boat for me when I had finished. Then I fell into bed, exhausted, and did not sleep at all.

The following day was another in a string of sticky summer dog days. Even with the air-conditioning, the heat pulsed through the cabin's fiberglass walls. I did some final straightening and then drove to the Y. It took a two-hour workout before I was able to expend the adrenaline borne of nervous anticipation. I went back to the boat, showered, had a salad, and waited.

It was a little after two when the phone rang. Michael and the kids were here. I walked to the hotel, which was only a short walk down the street. Through the glass of the lobby doors I saw them, sitting together in one of the large overstuffed chairs. Michael's eyes were closed, head back against the cushions. Joshua was nestled under one arm, sucking his thumb. Lizzie was sitting stiffly against her father's body, large eyes staring straight ahead. She saw me and I waved. Her expression did not change.

Great, I thought.

I opened the lobby door and was met with a rush of cold air. Michael's eyes opened and he struggled to rise, sliding both children to the side. I walked to him and he gave me a quick hug and a mild kiss on the cheek. He was trying to look casually friendly, but I could sense how tightly wound he was. I managed a smile.

"Hi! Good trip down?"

"If by good you mean endless and miserable, yes," he returned facetiously, then turned back to the children. "Lizzie, do you remember Miss Sandi?"

The child nodded seriously.

"Hi, Lizzie," I said softly, in what I hoped was a non-threatening voice. "I'm glad you could come to visit me. "

She said nothing, just continued to look at me with that same solemn expression. Joshua, apparently distressed at the lack of attention he was receiving, stood up in the chair and swung his fat wet fist toward me.

"Dis is my thumb," he announced proudly.

"So it is," I said.

Michael picked up the toddler and balanced him on one shoulder. Then he held out his hand to Lizzie.

"Why don't we let Miss Sandi show us her boat," he suggested.

Lizzie took his hand after a quick glance at me. I couldn't help but wonder if she was waiting for me to turn into some kind of baby-eating monster. She had that same wary look that prey always gets in the movies just before becoming the lunch of some immense prehistoric predator. In this way we set off toward the boat, me leading, Michael behind with children in tow.

Lizzie warmed a bit when she saw the boat. Everything in the cabin is really more suited to a child's size, and the long quarter berth which seems a claustrophobic fit for me was like a giant walled playpen to the children. I fed them a few selections from the legions of junk food I had purchased and gave them some toys. Joshua responded almost immediately by curling up and falling asleep. Lizzie had located my stack of *National Geographics* and settled into the back corner of the bunk, out of sight, to look at them while we talked.

Michael and I were probably less comfortable than the children. We stood awkwardly in the cabin, sipping cold light beers and remembering how we had made love here. We made small talk, discussing Michael's job, his parents, and the article I was working on. Somewhere along the way Lizzie also curled into a tight little fetal ball and fell asleep. We moved to the front stateroom and sat on the v-berth. Michael reached over and covered my hand in his.

"Don't worry about Lizzie. She takes a long time to warm up to people."

"I'm not worried," I lied.

"I can tell." He grinned, picking up a large rubber fish from the basket that sat on dresser. "This yours?"

"No, I bought it for them, so they'd have something to play with."

Michael hugged me and kissed the top of my head. "Thank you for making them feel welcome."

"You're welcome."

"Am I?" he asked, moving closer.

The sleeve of his shirt rubbed against my bare arm. He leaned forward and looked into my eyes seriously. My face grew warm and my breath came in shorter gasps. I tilted my head forward and our lips met.

The kiss was warm and soft, and it had the same awkward anticipation of the kisses we take as teenagers. I don't know if it was the presence of the children in the boat or the sense that this was becoming dangerous emotionally, but I felt both guilty and exhilarated. I drew back. Michael's eyes were closed and his lips still parted. I don't know when it happened that I had memorized every curve and line of his face, but in that moment I knew him as intimately as I knew myself. I touched both sides of his face, cupped my hands around them, and kissed him again.

When it is like this, it is magic. I had felt this magic with Ryan, and I believed it to be a rare gift, something we two had outside of the everyday world of man. Now, again, I felt that I had been struck through with a clear white bolt of lightning, and it stunned me. The slow degrees by which I had come to care about Michael were eclipsed by this white hot light. All of the considerations—his children, his wife—were turned to ash, meaningless and inconsequential as dust.

He finally drew back.

"Wow," he whispered.

I searched my mind for a light comment, but I couldn't do it. It would be too dishonest for what I was feeling.

"Wow," I answered.

Just then Joshua started to whimper. Michael smiled at me apologetically.

"Maybe later," he said. "I got us adjoining rooms, and they go to bed early."

I would have said that I had no intention of making love in the room next to his children, but I suspected that I had lost any vestige of willpower when he kissed me.

Joshua was cranking up to a full-fledged cry and little Lizzie was crawling out of the bunk. Michael went to both of them and hugged them.

"What do you guys say to swimming?" he suggested cheerfully.

They were too tired and grumpy from the short nap to express much enthusiasm, but Michael pressed forward with his plans, so I took this to be a fairly natural frame of mind for small children. He decided to take them back to change and meet me at the hotel pool. I agreed to pack up toys, snacks, and drinks. With this division of labor we were camped out at one of the umbrella-clad tables less than half an hour later.

The children did love the pool. Lizzie had a flotation jacket, but within the first twenty minutes it was unnecessary. She took to the water and swam gracefully. Joshua loved it as well, though his first mouthful when dunked provided a few minutes of tears and concern. I marveled watching Michael with them—a tall, handsome man, clearly devoted to his two beautiful children. I wondered if Liz had ever seen him this way, and how the things she said about their marriage could seem so foreign to the man I had come to know.

Lizzie was calling my name, asking me to watch as she attempted an underwater maneuver. I clapped in admiration and she smiled at me, the first real smile I had seen, wet hair plastered to her face, and I smiled back.

"You have a beautiful little girl," a woman said near me.

"Thank you," I said, and I meant it.

Later I would see this day as a kind of jewel, all bright and clear and impossibly precious. At the time I just knew that I felt a kind of satisfied happiness that I had not felt for so long that it was like I'd discovered a brand new emotion. We played together like children, Michael and I wrestling and splashing with Lizzie and Josh, and the sounds of water and laughter were like music. We showered and changed and went off to dinner in the same high spirits, and everything from Josh's expression when he saw a steamed crab to Lizzie's delight at her real cherry and tiny paper umbrella in her cherry coke were occasions of great joy. We walked back in the twilight swinging hands and talking, the soft evening breeze on our flushed faces.

Josh squealed with pleasure at the ducks perched on the shore by the marina entrance, their heads already tucked under their wings for an evening sleep. As he ran to chase them, Lizzie ran after him, and they both turned the corner ahead of us and disappeared.

I felt a little frisson of fear. I knew they were safe. There was no crime here. The water was still hundreds of yards away. Yet I found myself clutching Michael's hand tighter and pulling him along until we could see them again. *This is what parenthood means.*

"Is everything okay?" he asked, catching some change in my mood.

I summoned a smile and dismissed the phantoms from my mind. "Everything is perfect," I answered.

"I thought so too," he said and kissed me.

We walked the rest of the way back to the hotel together, Josh and Lizzie alternately scampering ahead and running back. When we reached the lobby, they rushed to one of the chairs and jumped on to the cushions. Michael laughed.

"It might take me awhile to put them down," he said. "Do you want to come back over in an hour or so?"

"Not tonight. I'm afraid you all have worn me out," I said.

He looked at me with both concern and disappointment.

"Just for tonight," I said, and I kissed his cheek. "I'll see you in the morning."

He squeezed my hand and smiled.

I said goodnight to the children. Joshua hugged me and gave me a sloppy kiss, and even Lizzie touched my cheek. The day felt like an unqualified success.

"I'll be back," I promised in my best movie imitation voice.

I considered it proof of just how much he cared for me that he found that funny. Still laughing, he slung both children over his shoulders and headed to the elevator. I watched them go and then headed back along the waterfront to my boat.

Absentee boaters and "Rivah house" owners had descended on the village in migrating flocks, and their summer presence kept the town alive. They were, on the whole, polite and genteel, so strolling couples and families people the streets late at night, eating ice cream cones and talking in low, contented voices. Music drifts from the few bars, but it is usually acoustic, accompanied by high, sweet singing that interweaves with the tourists to create something that smells and tastes like summer.

Perhaps this is why I am never afraid to be alone here. When I lived in a middle class, suburban neighborhood, the dark windows always seemed threatening, and unlocked doors were an invitation to disaster. I hated to take a shower when no one was home, always thinking I heard something, turning off the water, only to find while I stood there shivering that it was gone. Here I never locked the boat, and I biked to the store, my favorite restaurant, the art gallery, coffee shop, and bookstore, all without a second thought for my safety.

Tonight the docks were quiet. Knowing perhaps my penchant for being alone, the marina manager had given me a slip at the end of the farthest pier, surrounded by boats that were seldom used. I could see a few people in their cockpits on other docks, engaged in quiet conversation and sipping drinks, and a few waved as I passed.

I curled into my berth and slept with a sense of contentment that I had not known since Ryan was alive. But in the night, the dreams came again, only this time the face beneath the water was not Liz's face. It was the face of her beautiful five year-old child.

I knew then that they wouldn't stop until I found Debra Windler.

Chapter 27

THE PHONE RANG HALF-A-DOZEN times before Wayne picked up. It was Monday morning, and I had forced myself to wait until ten, but I found I couldn't eat or work. I just paced back and forth in the small space of the boat like a caged animal.

"Kremm," he said, voice sounding bleary and hungover.

"Is this the *Post* or the morgue?" I asked.

"San. Please, no feeble attempts at humor. Every time I move my head my entire office seems to rearrange itself. Have a heart."

"Sorry," I said contritely.

"That's a girl. So how was the grieving alleged widower and his horde?"

"I won't discuss your alcohol problem if you don't bring up my weekend," I responded.

Wayne seemed to perk up at this. "Trouble in paradise? Need a good shoulder to cry on?"

"No, I don't," I said, more sharply than I had intended. The weekend had been nearly perfect, but I could not escape the ominous warning of my nightmares.

"All right, I can take a hint. The weekend is off limits. Do you still want to know where to find the dear departed?"

I stiffened. "You found her?"

"In a manner of speaking. The little interns worked late Friday. They called about sixty law offices before we had a hit. Hold on, it's here somewhere..." I heard the sound of papers shuffling. "Ah, here we go. Brannigan and Sons.

Small firm in downtown Atlanta. She apparently was hired there in late March, and left about three weeks ago."

"She left? How does that help? She could be anywhere."

"Non, mon cheri," Wayne said in his worst imitation French. "It just gets better. One of my eager beavers got ahold of a rather, shall we say loose-lipped secretary? Your darling girl quit because she was bedding the Brannigan—not a son, the old man himself—and it was deemed unseemly by the general staff and partners."

"She was fired because she sleeping with the president of the firm?"

"Not fired, not at all. She resigned. And sleeping is not a suitable term for what was going on there. His wife of forty-three years kicks him out, the marriage is kaput, and he buys your Liz—excuse me, Debra—a mansion somewhere outside of town."

I was still a moment. "Do you mean to say," I asked slowly, "that Liz is living with this Brannigan guy?"

"Engaged to be married, dear heart," he responded cheerfully.

I didn't know what to say.

"It must have caused quite a stir," Wayne continued. "From what my girl said, the aforementioned secretary needed very little convincing to spill the beans. Apparently the entire legal community has been quite scandalized. The ex was an Old South deb, lineage going back to before the Civil War. She inherited all of her father's money, and basically set Brannigan up in the firm. They had three sons, all lawyers. She was the model socialite wife, big with charities, and he up and dumps her without so much as a warning. And the low-level paralegal is suddenly Mrs. Brannigan-in-training."

There was a long pause while I considered this. When he spoke, Wayne seemed to have lost his humor.

"I was going to call you when I got this, but you said to let it wait."

"I know. Thanks."

"So what are you going to do?"

I sighed. "I don't know."

I could feel him nodding. "Yeah, this is one screwed up situation. I want you to know, I will forget I ever heard any of this. As far as I am concerned, Liz Bryson is dead. End of story."

"Thanks, Wayne."

There was a pause.

"You're still not going to let this go, are you?" he said finally.

"No."

"I know you're going to say it's none of my business, but you need to rethink this.

If you go down there, you've lost all plausible deniability. It's not just a suspicion anymore. If the truth ever comes out and her husband finds out you didn't just think Liz was alive, you knew it without a doubt, then you won't be playing house anymore."

"So you don't think I should go."

"It's your call. But you need to think about what you want, what your goal is."

I had thought about it for most of the night.

"I guess I want to hear it from her myself—why she called me, why she left Michael, why she left those children. I want to know if she meant to do all of this or if she couldn't help it."

He sounded exasperated. "Why? What difference does it make whether she is crazy or not?"

For me, quite a bit. If Liz suffered from a mental disturbance so serious that she would do anything to escape it, then she likely still needed help. That meant she was unpredictable.

"I have to know if she is stable enough to continue as Debra Windler. If she is, fine. Let her. But if she isn't, who's to say she won't break down next week or even next year and decide she wants to go home?"

"I see your point. But what are you going to do, go ring Liz's doorbell and ask her if she's crazy? Either way, she'll probably take off the minute she sees you. Do you have any idea how many laws she's broken?"

I had a general idea.

"I don't think so," I said, ignoring the question. "It sounds like she worked out a good deal as Debra Windler. Why would she sacrifice all that unless she's sure it's necessary? If I were her, I'd wait and at least see what I wanted."

"Maybe," Wayne said uncertainly. "Or maybe she'll club you over the head with a bottle of chardonnay and bury you in the basement. I still think you need to reconsider before you go down there. Why not try a phone call instead?"

"I have to look in her face, Wayne. It's the only way I'll know."

He sighed. "All right. I've got some things I can't put off this week. If you wait until next weekend, I'll go with you.

I would have appreciated the back-up, but I knew I couldn't let the knowledge fester that long.

"No. The sooner the better. Did you get Brannigan's home address?"

"Sadly, no. And nothing is online except the old address. I'm sure they know at the office, but they weren't telling. You'll have to track it down once you get there."

"I'll think of something."

"I never doubted it," Wayne said in a tone that made it clear he wasn't joking. "Now, before you hang up, promise me you won't do anything foolish."

I thought about Michael.

"Too late," I said.

Chapter 28

I BOOKED A FLIGHT TO Atlanta for the following morning. I actually agonized over what to pack. It felt like some sort of party joke: What do you wear to confront the living dead? Or perhaps like a feature in one of those ridiculous fashion magazines that created headlines from nothing at all. I could see it now: "Fashion Tips for Amateur Detectives" or "Dressing to Confront Your Lover's Not-So-Deceased Wife." Such a dilemma, particularly in the Deep South in summer. It just seemed too dramatic an occasion for a sundress, and my wardrobe was woefully lacking in cool business wear. Of course, this debate, humorous as it was, kept me from the real question of whether I had perhaps lost my mind. The farthest from home I had gone from my boat since my move to Virginia was Pineyfield, and look where that had gotten me. I was chewing a fingernail and vacillating between a sleeveless black shift and a khaki short-sleeved suitdress when the phone rang.

It was Michael.

"I've been thinking about you."

"You just left last night," I said.

"That was hours ago. I got home here, and all I wanted to do was turn around and go back."

I felt that lurch in the stomach that comes just before getting on a ride at the amusement park or looking over the railing on a high balcony. Emotional vertigo, and I couldn't look down.

"Um," I said, for lack of anything better.

There was a pause.

"You don't sound too pleased. I thought...you might look at it as a good thing."

I was hanging between the absolute guilt of all I knew and didn't say and the wash of desire I felt for him. The smell of his skin, the feel of my hands against his chest, these were still too immediate to deny.

"I'm glad you miss me," I said softly. "I miss you, too."

"Why don't you drive up here for 4th of July weekend? We could go to the lake, hike out to Cooper's Rocks. The kids loved spending time with you."

"That sounds nice," I admitted.

"Then say yes."

What difference would it make? If my trip to Atlanta resurrected Liz, chances were good that I would never spend another night with Michael or ever again hug his children. A promise now would make him happy, and even if it were a lie it hurt no one and cost nothing.

It struck me then that I still cherished the hope Liz would tell me something to absolve her, some benign truth capable of making this secret a burden I could carry without guilt. Maybe she had known she was dying a slow and painful death and wanted to spare her family. Maybe she suffered from a psychosis so strong she had succumbed to a second, stronger personality, and really believed she was Debra Windler.

I know. It was a pitiful attempt at self-delusion, but it beat the truth.

"Yes," I said, though I was no longer certain of the question.

He breathed a sigh of relief. "I wasn't sure what else to say to convince you. You'll drive up that Friday? I can get off a little early."

"Sure."

"Then I'll email you the directions, and you can meet me at the plant. GPS is iffy here in the hills. Is that okay? That way you don't have to face the family alone if I'm a little late."

"Are they that bad?"

"No," Michael said encouragingly. "They're great. They're anxious to meet you. You know, they all think I need to start looking for a new wife right away—single fathers are an anathema back here. If I don't start showing up with someone, I'll be fair game for every neighbor's unmarried niece in town."

"So I'm just a distraction," I joked.

"You are distracting. I'll call you again Thursday night to check on everything, okay?"

"Sure. Sounds good. I'll talk to you Thursday," I said.

He hung up.

I finished packing. I looked across the cabin at my face in the mirror. It was just as well that Michael could not see it. The strain of lying was betrayed in the tight jaw and thin lips. I could not continue that way.

This was going to end, one way or another.

Chapter 29

I DROVE TO BWI AT seven-thirty the following morning. I parked in the overnight lot and checked in for a nine a.m. flight that was mercifully on time. I flew on Southwest because it was cheap, but the seats had the same stained stickiness of a Greyhound bus, and the other passengers all looked like walk-on's for the Jerry Springer Show. I sat beside a young woman of nineteen or twenty who had more hardware piercing her face than I had on the deck of my boat. Still, the flight was only an hour from boarding to touchdown, so I had no real grounds for complaint.

The air in Atlanta was scorching hot. My dress stuck to my thighs as soon as I stepped outside, and I dismissed any thought of a shuttle or subway ride. Instead, I hailed a cab to go downtown. I had booked a room at the Hilton across from Centennial Park. I had never been to Atlanta but I knew the Olympics had taken place there. The hotel's internet ad had boasted that it was in the center of the professional, business, and financial districts, and the map had shown it to be only a block or so from the offices of Brannigan and Sons.

I had read before that Atlanta was the rising spirit of the new South, but the scene that unfolded outside the cab windows was depressingly old. Homeless men crouched in alleys against the slight shade of buildings like vampires afraid of the light. We passed a beautiful green park with a fountain that flowed like a waterfall down a stepped wall, but every bench and tree served as the bed for an indigent soul lying with a newspaper spread open as a tent over his face and chest. Twice at stoplights someone approached the car, bottle in hand, eyes glazed and wild. I shrank back against the seat.

Finally the cab stopped in front of a high-rise hotel. The buildings in this section proclaimed their wealth—all at least fifty stories high with uniformed doormen—but the streets were still dirty and the homeless seemed to be posted like sentries, one every hundred feet or so. As I got out of the cab I noticed the overhead walkways, glassed-in, that ran between the buildings and over the stifling streets. The privileged, then, need never breathe the same air as these poor unfortunates, much less walk shoulder-to-shoulder with them.

I was ashamed of myself for feeling grateful.

I checked in with little difficulty, despite the fact that every clerk at the desk wore a tag which proclaimed an unpronounceable name as well as a place of origin far from the domain of the English language. My room was on the thirty-eighth floor and looked like hotel rooms the world over—two double beds with floral spreads in shades of maroon, pecan-finished furniture, nondescript prints, television and mini-bar. I opened the local entertainment guide and looked at the street map. It was nearly noon.

I had the office address but no home address. I didn't want to march into the office and confront Brannigan senior about his new fiancé—in fact, I wanted to avoid any contact with him at all. What I really wanted was a chance to see Liz at home without anyone else around. I think I still held on to this idea that there really was no Liz, that this had all been some sort of mistake. I half-hoped to go up to the door, ring the bell, and see a perfect stranger. In order to do this, I needed a door to go to. I checked the phone book and dialed Brannigan's office.

"Brannigan and Sons. How may I direct your call?"

It was a clear, no-nonsense voice. Still, it was young and possibly worth the chance.

"I really don't know. This is, um, sort of embarrassing."

"Excuse me?"

"Well," I said, forcing a higher voice than normal, "I don't really know who can help me. I need an address."

"The firm's address is 36457 Peachtree, the Sloane Building, Suite ninety-two," the voice said efficiently.

"Oh, I have that address," I said dramatically. "That's just the problem! I need the home address."

"Whose home address are you looking for?" the voice inquired, the southern accent creeping through along with the annoyance.

I don't know where I get these ideas. For someone who has lived a relatively honest and straightforward life, lying now seemed as natural as breathing. "Well, this really is embarrassing. See, a few weeks ago I worked one of those parties, you know? And she placed an order, but she never gave me a home address, and when I looked in the book, this was all I came up with."

Curiosity was getting the better of the receptionist. "You say you worked a party, and someone from the firm ordered something?"

"Yes, that's it," I said, allowing relief to color my tone. "It was one of those lingerie parties, you know? Not just lingerie. The company I represent has, you know, some sex toys, lotions, vibrators, stuff like that."

I could hear the sharp intake of air on the other end.

"Who exactly placed the order?" the receptionist asked, and I knew I had her.

"Well, here's the thing. She went on and on about how it was a surprise, and I got the idea that her boyfriend is kind of, you know, straight-laced, so I really hate to give a name."

She took the bait. "I can't help you without a name, ma'am."

This was as good as a promise. "Well, if you're sure you won't mention it..."

"Absolutely," she answered, and I swear I could hear her salivating.

"The customer's name is Debra Windler, but she charged it to the credit card of a Mr. Brannigan, so I assumed..."

I could feel her delight. "Mr. Brannigan's fiancée! Of course! My goodness!"

She actually giggled.

"Right, so you see my problem," I said. "I don't want to just show up at his office with this package."

"Absolutely. I understand completely. Hold one moment." I could hear her clicking away on computer keys. "Do you have a pencil and paper ready?"

"Right here."

"Okay, it's 4112 Parkhurst Terrace. That's over on the north side of town, in the suburbs—it's near the Gravely Country Club."

"Great! You're a lifesaver!" I emoted. "Please, please don't mention my call to Mr. Brannigan. I'd hate to lose a good customer."

"Not a problem," she answered. "My lips are sealed."

As I hung up I imagined her rushing to the closest cubicle to share the hot news. I wasn't worried. I didn't think anyone would be calling Debra Windler or mentioning my call to Mr. Brannigan.

I decided I didn't just want to show up with a cab at Liz's door. Under the circumstances, a little surveillance of the house would probably be a good idea, and that really couldn't be done with a cab. I called the hotel desk and got the number of a local car rental agency that would be more than happy to deliver. I decided on a nondescript navy sedan which the representative assured me would be in front of the hotel by seven a.m. tomorrow.

This left me most of the afternoon with nothing to do. A check of the tourist map showed a small section of shops and restaurants just a few blocks away. I changed into a clean pair of khaki shorts and a white t-shirt and shouldered the small leather backpack that I often use as a purse. Then I set off to explore.

The first glassed-in walkway ran from the third floor hotel lounge area to a high rise hotel across the street. This in turn led to another walkway that connected to a small indoor mall replete with a Brooks Brothers, a Kinko's, a beauty salon, and a variety of other businesses geared to the busy traveler. The whole place had an air of unreality, as if the city itself did not exist outside of these glass mazes. This is so different from the cities I love, Baltimore, Richmond, or New York, where the teeming life of the city permeates even the indoor spaces. Downtown Atlanta seemed bereft of the funky little sidewalk cafes and ethnic restaurants that are so much a part of other urban areas.

I crossed yet another glassed-in walkway and ended up in the third floor bedding section of a large upscale department store. I took the escalator down to the ground floor and wandered the cosmetic aisles, trying on perfume. I do not like to shop when I need something. For example, if I know I'm going to a dinner and I absolutely need a small, black evening purse, that is the worst type of shopping. On the other hand, shopping just to look—window-shopping—is fine. Ryan and I used to drive to Fredericksburg or Alexandria or Annapolis on quiet fall Sundays and wander the streets in the historic districts, marveling at expensive paintings or crystal statues which we loved but had no intention of buying. I can get lost in just looking.

I was musing about this while comparing two shades of lipstick when I saw her. I don't think I would have even recognized her if I had seen her coming toward me, full face, but I caught just the slightest glimpse out of the corner of my eye and it registered as a familiar image. I turned my head slowly.

She was at the counter perpendicular to mine, her back to me. Her hair was cut in a sleek honey-blonde bob. She had been leaning over, trying on eyeshadow, so her hair had fallen off of one side of her face and her silhouette was framed against a large black velvet display. It was the line of face, the forehead, nose, and generous mouth that registered with my subconscious. It looked nothing like her, yet I knew with absolute certainty it was Liz.

I looked away quickly. There is much to be said for the notion that someone staring at you draws your own eyes, and I wasn't prepared for her here. I moved off slowly, nonchalantly, until I was several counters away, obscured by mirrors. Pretending to peruse a case of wrinkle creams, I was able to watch her between the displays.

Definitely thin, thinner than I had ever seen her. She had that emaciated slimness, flat hips, and slightly protruding pelvic bones that infatuate fashion magazines. She wore a pale blue, sleeveless sheath, plain but clearly expensive, with a modest gold necklace and diamond earrings. Her make-up, at least what I could see of it, was tastefully done, just a hint of color, with sculpted brows and full dark lashes. If anyone had seen her in Paris or London they would have felt the same: here was a beautiful woman with money. She exuded it like a scent.

I tried to look at her and see the woman who had lived in that sad little neighborhood in Pineyfield, but I couldn't. The woman at the make-up counter did not look like a baby had ever spit up on her shoulder. She didn't look like she would even be seen cooking in a kitchen with nursery school papers beneath refrigerator magnets. It would be a stretch to see her cooking at all.

This was something else I hadn't counted on. I felt envy.

This woman had done what I would never have imagined—she reinvented herself as someone better, and it had worked. There was little of Elizabeth Bryson to be seen. It was as if her fairy godmother transformed her into a country club princess. How often have we all wished we were someone else, only to settle for the selves we are? She had literally rewritten the story of her birth.

She paid for purchases and turned her back to me, walking away. I followed her, staying well behind. She passed the jewelry counters and stepped out on to the sweltering Atlanta street. Seconds later a large, silver sedan pulled up and a driver got out quickly, opening the door for her and tucking her efficiently into the back seat. Long before I reached the glass doors, the car was gone.

Chapter 30

I WOKE EARLY. THE SUN had not risen, but the Atlanta sky was the permanent light gray of a city that can never see stars. I dressed in the sheath and sandals, little jewelry or make up. I didn't even try to rehearse what I was going to say. I erased my mind completely.

The car was delivered, a nondescript sedan, and I headed to the suburbs. I had pinpointed the address on an Internet map the previous night at the hotel, and except for a few unexpected excursions in the wrong direction on a one way street, I arrived on Liz's street before seven forty-five a.m.

The houses were large, McMansions on miniature lots that probably sold for a million dollars each. The lawns were all manicured with underground sprinkler systems and perfectly sculpted bushes. The few flowers that could withstand the Atlanta heat were out of place, like bright splotches of some tropical drink spilled accidentally on the carpet of dry green. Liz's house looked much like the others, only somewhat larger. It was a house in the Georgian style, with pillars in the front and a formal brick driveway. I pulled up across the street from the house next door and waited.

About fifteen minutes passed and a gray sedan pulled up. It was the same one I had seen Liz get into the day before. No one got out; instead, the front door opened and a tall, gray-haired man in a gray suit came out carrying a briefcase. As he approached, the driver's door opened, but he waved the driver back inside, climbed in the back seat, and they pulled away. I assumed this to be Mr. Brannigan senior.

Now that the time had come, I really didn't know what to do. I suddenly felt foolish. Who did I think I was? I could not be an avenging angel, because I had nothing to avenge. The wrong done to me did not justify the effort I had put into tracking Liz and finding the truth. The only possible explanation was my connection to Michael, and being here did more to endanger that relationship than to ameliorate it.

In the end, it was probably nothing more than curiosity that led me up the curved brick walkway to the massive oak door.

I rang the bell and waited.

There were footsteps, distant and approaching on a hard tile floor. There was the sound of a deadbolt turning and the door swung open quickly.

"Did you forget your—"

The woman stood, frozen. It was obvious that she expected Brannigan. She stared at me as if just gradually registering my facial features. Her eyes widened briefly, and then something like amusement tugged at the corners of her mouth.

"Well," Liz said. "This is a surprise. Would you like to come in?"

I had expected many things: perhaps denial, a pretense of unrecognition, a feigning of amnesia, but certainly not this. I had even privately cherished some notion that she might break into tears of remorse at my sudden appearance. My own role as the hand of justice in these fantasies temporarily suspended, I nodded mutely, unable to think of a single syllable worth uttering, and followed her inside.

The house was large and airy in the way of these new luxury houses. High ceilings and marble tile, expanses of white plaster and magnificently carved staircase, even the upholstered Louis XVI chairs seemed carefully chosen to complete the image of culture and centuries-old class. A gilded mirror, at least four feet wide and five feet high, reflected my pale face as we passed.

Liz turned into a short, bright hallway that opened into a glassed-in sunroom. It was furnished with overstuffed chairs and loveseats in a pale chintz. Liz settled on the pillowed loveseat and motioned for me to sit on the chair adjacent her. I sat. We still had not spoken.

She looked at me for a moment. I met her eyes, but I felt uncomfortable and looked away, feeling unaccountably guilty.

"Would you like a Bloody Mary or a cup of coffee?" she asked in the tone one takes for a social call.

"No, thank you," I said stiffly.

She gestured at her own glass, half full of red liquid and garnished with celery, sitting on the glass-topped table beside her.

"You don't mind if I finish this?"

"No."

She took her glass, twirled it once between her fingers, and took a sip thoughtfully. Up close, I could see more of the features I remembered— the full lips, the wide face and large, vivid eyes. But the high cheekbones that now defined her had once been hidden beneath layers of fat, and the porcelain skin had never seemed as translucent as now, set off by the pale hair. I always thought of her as a pretty woman, even when overweight, but now, weighing no more than a hundred and twenty pounds at most, she was truly stunning.

"I wondered, sometimes, if you would go this far," she said musingly. "I didn't really think so."

"You left a trail," I said. "I just followed it."

Liz threw back her head and laughed. It was not a pleasant sound, but harsh and high.

"I think it was more than that," she said, shaking her head. "I didn't exactly leave a forwarding address."

Yes," I agreed quietly, "it was more than that. You shouldn't have called me."

Liz smiled a bit ruefully. "I see that now. Don't misunderstand, Sandi. I called you because I thought you were the perfect person to handle my death. If I left a trail, it wasn't intentional. I was not sitting here in Atlanta waiting to be found."

"I didn't think you were."

She laughed as if I had told a joke, but I kept my face cold and impassive. She reached out and patted my knee with her hand, and I flinched away involuntarily. She sat back on the loveseat and sipped the drink again, her face pensive.

"Well, then," Liz said curiously, as if the answer did not affect her, "what exactly do you want? Money?"

"No," I said, stung. "I didn't come here to blackmail you."

"Then what exactly did you see yourself doing here?" she asked, her voice suddenly hoarse with anger. "Were you going to show me the error of my ways and reunite me with my husband? Did you bring baby pictures to inspire guilt? Do you expect me to go the police and make a full confession? Or did you just want to make sure I wasn't coming back?"

My face must have betrayed the answer.

"Ah, so that is it, is it?" The outburst of emotion was gone, and if anything, she sounded vaguely amused. "Well, you have no worries there.

Liz Bryson is dead—deader than a doornail, to quote Dickens—but unlike the ghosts, I won't be coming back. I am Debra Windler. There is no going back."

"But the children—" I began.

"Don't!" she exploded, again releasing the turmoil that lay just beneath the current of conversation. "Don't pull that out. It's not like I just walked out on them. I died to make it easier on them."

"But you didn't die," I said softly.

"Really? That's not what the papers said. I am dead to them, to the state of Maryland, and to the insurance company. To everyone whose opinion of me will matter to Michael and the children. End of story."

She was calm again and lay back against the cushions, drinking.

I leaned forward, exasperated. 'You make it sound so simple. It wasn't simple for Michael, or for your children, or for me. Do you have any idea how hard this has been for everyone? Do you understand that a man was arrested for your murder and that he took his own life? How can you just dismiss that?"

"Don't lecture me about Bernie Wathen," she said sharply. "He got what he deserved. He was a coward and a liar. Besides which, I understand you had a hand in that. As for Michael and the children, you have no idea what you are talking about, so don't tell me how hard it was for them. Living together was hard for them, and I imagine that they all feel better off."

I wasn't going to argue that point, since it was too close to the truth.

"All right," I said finally. "I'm not lecturing. I just want to understand, okay? I want to know why you called me and basically dragged me into this whole... farce, why you felt that this was your best option out of all of choices you had. Explain it to me."

"You are a priest, now? You want to hear my confession, is that it? You want me to ask for absolution?"

I suppose I did.

Liz was watching me carefully, and when I did not answer, she smiled a slow, cat-like smile, unlike any I had ever seen on her face. It was almost unnerving.

"I wish I could say that I planned it all out with you playing this very interesting part, but I didn't. Does that disappoint you? I'm afraid you were a last minute addition. I wondered later if maybe I was overreaching with you, but I knew how anal you could be about details, and I thought you might make sure that Bernie didn't just walk off scot free. I was looking for a little public humiliation for him—I didn't think you'd have him arrested for murder."

I looked at her in surprise. "You didn't plan to frame him for your murder? You must have known how it would look—the blood in your car, the fight that you had had."

"The blood was unexpected. I taunted him, I couldn't help it. I had grown to feel such hatred of him, that when I knew I was going to be gone, I... well, it hardly matters what I said. I didn't think he would actually hit me. I didn't think he was even that much of a man. So the blood was mine."

"He said you were upset because he was breaking it off."

Her laugh was high and tight. "Did he? It was pure pride on my part. The plan had been made. I didn't need him anymore for anything. But the fact that he was ending it because he was too much of a coward to stand up to his wife and his buddies at the Moose lodge or wherever the hell he went. Here I was going to be dead in twenty-four hours, and he picked this time to dump me. I was insulted."

"The plane tickets?"

"That was a nice touch, don't you think?" she sounded pleased with herself. "He deserved it. People needed to know what he was, what he did."

"He wasn't the only one who was hurt."

"If you mean dear Mrs. Wathen, I wanted his wife to find out. I wasn't his first, you know. He specialized in manipulating young women with unhappy marriages and small children. One of them—a first year teacher from some backwoods town in North Carolina—actually did try to kill herself a few years ago. It was all hushed up, of course. You should have gotten a taste of Pineyfield hypocrisy from your visit there."

I nodded. "So he was a real rat. I get that. Don't you think the punishment was a little severe?"

"No. I didn't kill him. Neither did you. "

"What about Michael? Didn't you think it might hurt him to find out you were sleeping with another man?"

Liz didn't answer.

"All right. I understand about Wathen, but what about me, Liz? I still don't understand why you brought me into this. We hadn't even talked in what—nearly three years?"

Liz turned her head, looking past me at the pool water glistening like hard diamonds in the sun. "You'll laugh at this. The irony of it. After everything, I still cared about Michael. Not like I had, not enough to want him for myself, but enough to feel responsible for him. All of those years when I gained weight, saw therapists, I felt so weak. Later, when I realized that he was weak, too, that he needed me to be weak because he couldn't handle me any other way, I felt sorry for him. He wasn't the right husband for me, but I wasn't much of a wife. "

It was the first thing she said that sounded like the woman I had known.

She took another sip of her drink, glanced at me, then resumed. "You don't understand, do you? Bringing you in made it easier because I knew Michael would fall in love with you."

This was not the answer I expected. My face flushed.

"That's ridiculous. There's no way you could predict that."

"No? You are everything I wasn't. You would make such a good mother, so responsible, steady, independent, and always keeping the stiff upper lip. Even when Ryan died, you gave yourself what, a week? A week to fall apart, and then you picked yourself up and acted as if it never happened. Do you know that you never even mentioned his name again to me? And I might have been your best friend."

"That's not true! You know how unhappy I was—"

'I know. But you never told me."

I digested that in silence. It did not seem true to me, but then again, I knew I had withdrawn into myself following Ryan's death.

"But since you're here, I guess that didn't work out as well as I had planned either."

My face grew red. Liz raised herself up on one elbow and laughed again.

'My God you have a transparent face. You never did play poker, did you? So, perhaps it wasn't such a bad idea after all."

We sat in silence then, she sipping the blood-red drink, me staring at her. I felt both fascinated and sickened. She reminded me of a carnivorous flower, beautiful to look at, but with a vicious cruelty at the core.

"You think I am a monster, don't you?" Liz said musingly. "It's not Bernie or even Michael. It's the children, isn't it? Only a monster would do this to her children."

I didn't answer.

She smiled humorlessly. "I can't explain it to you. You have to experience it to understand. Do you know what it's like to feel every day, every time you get in the car, that you just want to let the wheel go and close your eyes, that you would welcome the crash, the nothingness and emptiness of death? That I thought about drowning each one of those children just so

I couldn't hear their screaming? That I looked at Michael and I didn't even feel hate anymore—I felt an absolute void? I could not pretend to be the good wife, the good mother anymore. I just couldn't."

"Everyone gets depressed. When Ryan died—"

"No. Ryan's death didn't leave you with nothing, Sandi. You at least knew it had been good once. It was never good for us. Never. You had the memories of someone who loved you. I had, what? A husband who didn't love me, children I didn't want, and always this same feeling of despair, day in and day out. It wasn't a phase or a stage, Sandi. It was my life, every minute, from the alarm in the morning until I finally fell asleep at night. It was real."

"You could have gotten a divorce," I said. "You could have gotten help."

"Help! The only help I got were so many pills that I was like one of the Stepford wives. The psychiatrist said I didn't like myself. There was a shock! I was fat and unhappily married with dirty diapers and leaking breasts. I wasn't anything I wanted to be. How could I have liked myself? And the divorce lawyers... do you think either one of us could have raised those children on half the money? I was trapped. The way I saw it, I had two choices, and both of them were dying," she said, raising her glass to me as if in a toast. "I thought I'd try this way first. The other option is always open."

Beneath her brittle exterior, the despair was still there. I could hear it in her voice. She might have changed the face, the image she presented to the world, but I didn't think she liked herself any better. In spite of myself, I felt sorry for her, and I saw how what she had done could be justified in her own eyes.

"Are you really happier now?"

The question slipped out, an extension of my thoughts.

She rose with a sharp, quick movement, and gestured to the pool and the manicured gardens visible through the glass. "Shouldn't I be?"

"It's beautiful here, yes. But to me it seems like you have traded one cage for another," I pointed out.

Her expression darkened. "How poetic. Do you really believe that kind of drivel, or do you just say it when you're feeling self-righteous? It's all cages, Sandi. Realize that, and you're free to look for the best one."

"You don't love this lawyer?"

"You are too precious!" Liz said, allowing a southern accent to creep into her voice. "I love this house. I love my clothes. I love that he wants to fly me to exotic places and that he thinks I am the sexiest thing he has ever seen. Is that good enough for you?"

I shook my head.

"Well, there you go," she said simply. "Sure you don't want a drink?"

"I... I really don't know what to do," I said, which probably wasn't the smartest thing to say under the circumstances, though it had the virtue of being true.

I did not look at her when I said it, but I felt her grow still. There was a long pause.

"Well, are you thirsty?" she said finally.

I looked up and saw that she was smiling, though it was a bitter smile.

"You know what I meant."

Liz walked across the room, her back to me, and stood behind a small desk. Her voice was flat when she spoke.

"You know Michael. If you tell him about me, he'll go to the police."

I did know him. I knew he would be torn between perpetuating the lie and protecting his children. Even if he did not expose Liz, the dishonesty would eat away at him.

I knew then that I couldn't tell him.

"He'll never know," I said.

She looked at me for a long moment.

"Do you really think you can keep this to yourself?"

"I do. I love them."

Liz sighed and I heard the desk drawer, which she must have opened, slide closed. She moved toward the front door.

"I don't suppose we will keep in touch," she said.

I shook my head. "Probably not."

I followed her to the door. She stepped aside as I walked out.

Neither one of us said goodbye.

I got in the car and looked back as I drove away. She watched me go, a beautiful blonde woman framed by white columns, looking like an advertisement for the American dream in the mid-morning sun.

It wasn't until the next morning, on the plane to Virginia, that I thought to wonder what had been in the desk drawer.

Chapter 31

I LAY IN THE SUN, a sheen of sweat on my browned skin. The heat was oppressive, a force that held me still and unmoving against the plastic webbing. My eyes were closed, but the light behind my eyelids was still bright. It was low tide, exposing a strip of sand at the marina's grassy point where locals could pretend, at least for a few hours, they were at the beach. Their sounds drifted around me: children splashing in the river, the low, drowsy murmur of adult conversation, and the soft sound of footsteps, but I could not will myself to open my eyes.

"So, you are alive."

The chaise lounge lurched as a body perched on its edge beside me. The voice was Wayne's.

"Tell me this is just a bad dream," I said.

"You don't deserve a friend like me, do you know that?" he asked rhetorically. "Do you know I've emailed you every day this week? And do you ever check your voice mail?"

I opened one eye and peered at him guiltily.

"Sorry. Did you need me for something?"

He shook his head, exasperated. Even now, in the worst heat and humidity of a scorching summer day, Wayne wore dark pants and a long-sleeved shirt.

"I didn't need anything. I was worried about you."

"I'm touched," I joked, but I patted his leg at the same time, aware that he really did look worried.

"You are hopeless. The last I heard, you mounted your white horse and went to fight on the side of truth and justice in Atlanta. By now I would have assumed you were dead except I had one of the interns check to see that you got on a flight home."

I sat up, laughing. "All right, I am definitely guilty as charged. I didn't even think you might be worried. I really am sorry."

Wayne nodded, mollified. "You should be. Now, I expect you to tell me everything. Spare no small detail."

So I told him how I had found her, what we had said to each other, and how we had left it. When I finished, he let out a long breath.

"I wasn't far off, was I?" Before I could answer, he said, "Look, can we get out of this sun before I melt? Does that tub of yours have any air conditioning?"

"Yes, of course it does. Come on, I'll get you a drink. You know, you could always dress for the weather," I pointed out, rising.

"I am. Indoor weather, seventy point six degrees."

He followed me from the small beach to my dock, making several lecherous comments about my butt in a bathing suit which I tactfully ignored. We climbed aboard and slid into the cabin, which was cool and dark. I grabbed two light beers from the fridge and we sat on the sofas opposite each other. Wayne took a long appreciative sip.

"Much better. Now, let me ask you something. Do you have any clue just how dangerous that was?"

"What?"

"Confronting the lioness in her own den. She hasn't exactly shown herself to be above moral reproach. How did you know she wouldn't hit you over the head with the espresso machine and bury you in the back yard?"

I hadn't known this, hadn't really considered it until the plane ride home, but since then it had been on my mind.

"I didn't. I think..." I paused here, considering how much to say. "I think perhaps she had a gun in the desk drawer."

"What?" Wayne very nearly exploded. "She had a gun?"

"I don't know," I said quickly, defensively. "I didn't even think about it at the time, but later... the way she stood there, how she opened the drawer without me seeing. She wanted to know what I was going to do. She closed it when I said I wasn't going to tell Michael. Later, I wondered what she would have done if I had said something else."

"I have a pretty good idea," Wayne said disgustedly.

We sat in silence for a few minutes.

"So what are you going to do?"

"What can I do?" I asked. "It doesn't fix anything if I tell anyone about her; it only makes it worse for everyone."

"By everyone, you mean you?"

I scowled. "No, that's not what I mean. I mean Michael, his children, and anyone else who cared about her."

"Don't you think Bernie Wathen's family has a right to know?" he asked.

"This doesn't exactly exonerate him," I pointed out. "He was still an adulterer."

"That is somewhat less serious than being a murderer."

There was no response for that, so I gave none. We sat in a silence which I finally broke.

"What would you do?"

Wayne's face wrinkled into a grin.

"Publish it, write a book, make a fortune. But that isn't what you want to know. You mean, what would I do if I were you."

I nodded.

"Probably nothing."

Since that was exactly what he had just chastised me for doing, I felt justifiably irritable.

"I thought you said—"

"We were discussing moral rights and wrongs, not realistic actions," he said amicably. "If you tell Michael any of it, your relationship with him is over. Not that this would break my heart any, but it might break yours. I only have two concerns."

"Go ahead," I said.

"First, can you really keep it quiet? You've always struck me as disappointingly truthful, despite your recent foray into detective work. What if things work out for you? Could you keep a secret like this twenty years down the road?"

I hoped that I could, but I didn't honestly know the answer, so I shrugged. Wayne smiled and raised his bottle in a mock toast.

"Exactly."

I cleared my throat as he sipped his beer.

"What was the second thing?"

He appeared suddenly serious.

"Suppose she isn't so sure either?"

Chapter 32

MICHAEL CALLED LATER THAT SAME evening. I walked to a little café in town and had just finished eating alone at one of the back tables. I hadn't spoken to him since I'd gotten back from Atlanta, and I wasn't sure I could keep what I had seen out of my voice. Wayne was right in that I was basically truthful, although less from any moral scruple than because my emotions and thoughts tended to show plainly on my face. As Liz had said, I am not much of a poker player.

"You're still coming next weekend?"

"Absolutely."

I could hear the relief in his voice. "I wasn't sure. I thought maybe you changed your mind."

"No. I wouldn't miss it."

He asked about my week, but I turned the conversation to the children, and he told me how much they had talked about their visit, and how Lizzie had started drawing elaborate pictures of boats with stick figure families on board that looked suspiciously like all of us. I did not mention the trip to Atlanta, and if he heard anything unusual in my voice, he did not mention it. Instead he sounded truly happy, and I let his mood carry me with him. By the end of our conversation, I felt with absolute certainty that everything was going to be all right.

Which is often the first sign, at least in my life, that things are going to go terribly wrong.

Nick, the café owner, brought me the bill just as I hung up. He is about sixty, a former stock broker from the city who had decided rather suddenly that opening a restaurant was a good retirement job. His marriage lasted less than a month down here in the tidewater, a fact that did not seem to bother him in the least. He had a great sense of humor and made the best crab mac and cheese I have ever tasted, which explains why we were on a first name basis.

"Storm's coming," he said. "Did you walk?"

"Of course. I didn't see anything on radar when I left."

"Just popped up. There's a tornado watch, too. If you go now, you should make it back."

I gave him my credit card and followed him up to the bar, where he rang me out. I could see the sky through the front window, a dark grayish purple to the south in sharp relief against the low evening sun.

"That does look bad," I agreed.

"You want a ride? I can get Jimmy to run you home."

Jimmy was the busboy, all of sixteen, with a penchant for squealing tires.

"No thanks. I should be fine."

Nick grinned, undoubtedly aware of Jimmy's reputation behind the wheel.

"Probably smart. Take care."

The view from the street was reassuring—I had watched my share of storms come across the water, and this one looked to be at least a half-hour away, more than enough time to get to the boat and secure things. Still, I shouldered my purse and jogged back, just to be safe. By the time I reached the dock the wind had picked up, and all of the boaters and strolling tourists had taken cover. When I got to my boat I was surprised to see a small runabout tied behind me. It was one of the hotel's rentals, and it was unusual for those to dock here. Perhaps it had experienced engine trouble, I thought, and walked closer to take a look. Between the wind, the clanging of halyards, and the building waves crashing against the shore, I did not hear her come up behind me. I did not know she was there until I felt the cold metal against my thin shirt.

You don't have to have much experience with guns to recognize what one feels like when it is pressed into your back.

"Get in the boat," Liz said.

There were a lot of things I could have done then, I suppose. I didn't think of any of them. Instead, I carefully climbed down into the open cockpit of the little speedboat. She followed behind me, the gun pointed at my chest as I turned to face her.

Her blonde hair was pulled back from her face and covered with a baseball cap. She wore sunglasses, a dark shirt, shorts, and deck shoes, the uniform of the Northern Neck tourist. I could not read her expression.

"Untie the lines," she said.

"We can't go out in this," I said, and I heard my voice shake.

"Now," she said, waving her gun at me.

I untied the lines, holding the boat against the dock. She started the engine, still facing me, and gestured for me to push the bow off. As I did, she put it in gear and we headed straight out toward the channel. Beyond the mouth of creek, I could see the Rappahannock was churning with breaking waves and blowing spray.

The noise of the outboard and the wind nearly drowned out her voice, but the gesture of the gun was clear.

"Go sit on the front."

I worked my way around her and sat in the bow, clutching the handrail as the boat bucked into the chop of the creek.

"What do you think you're doing? You're going to get us both killed!" I shouted.

She pushed down the throttle, and the boat jumped up on a plane, pointing straight toward the river. I slid closer to her, raising my voice above the chaos.

"I already told someone about you!"

She pulled the throttle back, and the sudden deceleration nearly threw her into the windshield. I pushed myself up, but the gun was there again before I could reach her. We stood, facing each other in, only a foot or two apart.

"What did you say?" she asked, voice grim.

"Wayne Kremm. He's a reporter for the *Post*, he knows the whole story, he's the one who found you for me," I said, my words tumbling over each other in my haste to get them out.

"You dumb bitch," Liz said with disgust. "You trusted a fucking reporter?"

"He's a friend. He won't tell anyone unless something happens to me."

Liz slammed the gun against the dash.

"How can anybody be so stupid! Of course he'll tell. That's what people do. That's what you did!"

She slammed down the throttle and I fell backward, my head hitting the hard fiberglass seat as I fell, and then there was nothing.

It could have only been a few minutes, but my first conscious sensation was that of rain pelting down on my face. The wind was turning from the south to northwest, the boat twisting back and forth as it fought the disorganized seas, bruising my body as it crashed from side to side. I opened my eyes. Lightning flashed, followed almost simultaneously by a crash of thunder. I pushed myself up on my elbows and looked around.

We were heading toward the bridge and the deepest channel. Liz was still at the helm, the gun pressed against the windshield as she clutched them both, trying to steady herself at the wheel. There was no way to get to her before she could shoot me. I laid back against the floor and closed my eyes. The fear that I had felt when she first forced me into the boat was gone, replaced by an emotionless, practical calm that I did not recognize. I understood two things: I would have to wait for a better opportunity. And in all probability, I was going to die.

Our speed was slowing again.

"Get up!" Liz shouted.

I opened my eyes. She stepped toward me, gun pointed down at my body, and kicked at my legs. The sunglasses were gone now, and I could see her mascara and foundation running, as if her face had begun to melt in the rain. I scooted backwards against the seat and pushed myself up until I was sitting. When she saw I was done, she backed behind the windshield again and reached under side cowling, eyes still on me.

We were perhaps thirty feet from the concrete pilings of the Norris Bridge. The water here was flatter, the wind variable at no more than eight knots. I glanced behind me. Liz had outrun the worst of the storm, but I could see the wind line and dark sky behind me. It was coming for us, no more than a mile away.

"Get in the water," Liz said, tossing me an orange life preserver.

I looked at her in surprise.

"You're having an accident," she said. "You were out in your kayak, got caught in the storm, and fell overboard. Unfortunately, you must have been hit by a boat in the dark."

I understood then. The life preserver was a target. She intended to run me over.

"The only thing stopping Wayne from running a story about you is me," I said. "If you kill me, he'll come after you, whether he thinks you did it or not."

She shook her head. Her eyes were hard.

"You just don't get it, do you? I am not giving this up. Now that I know who he is, I can go after—"

I wasn't listening to her. The wind was rushing over the water behind me, a strong northwesterly gust, gaining force as she spoke. She heard it too, and her eyes widened as the squall hit the boat, cutting off her voice and tearing the hat from her head. She dropped the gun and reached for the dash with both hands as the bow rose up but she missed, her hand latching onto the throttle instead. As she fell backward, the boat was thrust into full reverse, and suddenly the concrete piling was racing toward the stern. I climbed up and pushed myself over the bow, kicking off as hard as I could, and dove into the river. Even before I surfaced, an explosion shattered around me as the motor and gas tank hit the bridge at thirty miles an hour. There was a fireball, impossibly bright in the near darkness, followed by a heavy plume of acrid smoke. There was no boat left, only pieces of fiberglass and blackened boat cushions, moving out with the tide, tossing up and down on the waves.

I did not think Liz could have survived, but I was not willing to stake my life on it. I swam away from the wreckage, letting the waves push me as I stroked toward the southern shore.

Chapter 33

I CAME ASHORE AT THE marshy tip of Locklies Creek.

The moon had risen about an hour before, providing enough light to walk the muddy shoreline. No houses were here at the mouth, but I could make out a dock about a hundred yards away. As I got closer, I saw a fuel pump at one end and a few crab boats tied to the posts. A small bait store was on the shore with an empty gravel parking lot. It was close to midnight then, clear and cool now that the front had passed through, and I was shivering and miserable. I am a good swimmer with no fear of the water, and I had never doubted that I could make the distance to land. Still, the breaking waves had threatened more than once to choke me, and my imagination had tortured me in the inky black stillness that followed. I was repeatedly stung by sea nettles as their wispy tendrils wrapped around my legs while I swam. Other things had brushed against me, too, larger things for which I had no name.

I found an unlocked restroom on the side of the store. The light switch turned on a single, dim bare bulb, but at least it worked. The sink was rusty and the toilet crusted with filth, but there was clear, hot water at the faucet that smelled only faintly of sulphur. I stripped off my clothes and used my shirt as a washcloth, sponging myself clean. I rinsed and wrung out my wet shorts and t-shirt as best as I could and put them back on. Then I put down the toilet seat, leaned my head against the wall, and fell asleep sitting there.

I woke to the sound of men talking and crab pots being unloaded. I was stiff and sore, and it took me several minutes to get up and stretch out enough to move without limping. I rinsed my face again. My clothes were still damp, and I could only imagine how I looked, given that there was no mirror. I opened the door and stepped out into the bright sunlight.

There were four men, ranging in age from perhaps eighteen to at least sixty, though their tanned and weathered faces looked much the same. They stopped talking as soon as they saw me.

"I had an accident on the river last night," I said. "Do any of you have a phone I can use?"

"You were out they-ah in the rivah las' night?" the largest of the watermen asked.

I had decided, sometime during the long hours in the water, that I would tell no one what happened until I knew if Liz were alive. Instead, I used the story she had given me.

"I was kayaking out past Carter's Creek and got caught in the storm," I said.

This revelation spurred them to action. I was led to the store, where the owner called his wife at their house down the street and instructed her to fetch some hot food and a blanket, and soon I was eating eggs and bacon while the anxious men took turns pressing a cup of hot coffee into my hands.

"Did you see the boat what blew up?" the youngest man asked.

"Ricky, don't you worry the poor girl with questions like that!" scolded Mrs. Swann, the owner's wife, a plump woman with rough hands and a kind face.

"It's all right," I said. "I did see something, some kind of explosion, but I was already in the water."

"I don't know how you stood it, swimmin' at night out there with God knows what," Mr. Swann said with a trace of admiration in his voice.

"Leastways, yer lucky you was clear of it. Some woman from over at the hotel had one of them rental boats out on the rivah, and she done plowed right into the cee-ment and blowed herself up," Ricky said.

"Was she... was she killed?" I asked.

"Kilt? I guess so, since she was blowed into bits," he exclaimed.

"I mean... are they sure? Was there any body?"

Mrs. Swann patted my arm. "You're thinking that her body was out there floating around in the river with you, aren't you? No, dear. The rescue boat got out there not long after it happened. They found what was left of her just under the water, pinned up against the concrete with some of the wreckage. It's just a shame they didn't find you."

I breathed slowly, in and out, to still the rapid beat of my heart. She was dead. It was over.

"Billy here is going to take you home," Mrs. Swann said, pointing to a middle-aged man standing in the doorway. "He has the engine shop next door."

I tried to protest that I could call someone, but Billy insisted.

"I got a delivery to make over there either way. It's no trouble."

And so it was that an hour later I was taking a hot shower on my boat, relieved to find my purse, slightly damp but otherwise intact, still on the cockpit cushion where I had thrown it the night before.

I was edgy with adrenaline and bad memories, and the only person I could talk to was Wayne. I called him twice, but both calls went straight to voicemail. I found myself pacing back and forth in the cabin, unable to sit still, when the phone finally rang.

"Not that I am not thrilled to hear from you, but eight a.m. is a little early, even for you," he said.

I launched into what had happened without any introduction, interrupted only by Wayne's occasional exclamation of horror or disbelief. I left out Liz's threat against him, if that is what it was, and ended with the words of the waterman and Mrs. Swann, which elicited a sharp intake of breath, followed by silence.

"Well?" I said.

"For once in my life, Sandi, I am speechless. I mean, completely without words," Wayne said. "You're sure you're all right? Shouldn't you go to the doctor, just to check things out?"

"No, I'm fine. A few scrapes, a rash where I was stung, but nothing I would need a doctor for," I assured him.

"Do you know if they identified the body yet?"

I hadn't thought about that. Perhaps this wasn't over yet, after all.

"Let me check it out," Wayne said. "I'll call you back in a half-hour."

He called me back even sooner than that.

"It's over," he said, sounding jubilant.

"What do you mean?"

"The woman was identified as Debra Windler. According to the police, she was staying at the Inn. That's where she rented the boat. When they searched her room, they found she had purchased several wooden decoys—some guy down your way hand carves them, and I understand they're pretty pricey. Apparently her fiancé collects those things. He has already released a statement saying that she told him she was going to

Virginia to get him a special wedding gift and mourning her tragic loss. The police already ruled it an accidental death. No autopsy, no DNA check. Liz Bryson won't be coming back from the dead this time."

I breathed slowly, in and out, letting his words sink in.

"You should be happy. This solves your problem completely," Wayne said.

I sat down and leaned my head back against the cushions. I closed my eyes.

"Sandi? Are you still there?"

"Yeah. I'm here."

"Are you all right?"

I wasn't. Where there should have been relief, there was only an aching sadness.

"I don't know what's wrong with me," I said plaintively.

"You've been through a lot. Hell, I'd probably have a nervous breakdown if it were me. Get some rest. I'll call you later this afternoon to see how you're doing."

I went back to the V-berth and lay down. Wayne was right, my problem was solved. Liz was truly gone, and what difference did it make if her death had happened months ago or last night? I could go to Michael now without the constant fear that she might somehow resurface and destroy our lives. It could not be wrong for two people who had lost as much as we had to find happiness in each other.

Right, wrong, good, evil. They weren't concepts I had ever spent much time considering until now. If you had asked me a week before, I would have said I did not believe in evil. People are fragile and weak, but more often than not, the wrong that they do is for a right reason. After last night, I was not so sure. There was a darkness to Liz, a lack of empathy, that was, if not evil, the beginning of evil. Was that same seed in all of us, waiting for the right circumstance to germinate and grow? What had allowed it to flourish in a woman I had once called my friend?

I thought back to what Michael told me about their marriage. Liz's claim that she was pregnant when she was not.

I knew then where the evil had begun. It had started with a single lie.

That is when I knew I could not go to Michael.

I could not tell him about Liz, and I could not share a life with him that began with a lie. I could not know all that I knew and keep it hidden from him without some cost. No matter how pure my intentions, in the end, it would poison us as surely as Liz's lie had poisoned them.

I picked up the phone.

Epilogue

IT IS FALL NOW. THE leaves are turning, and there is that crisp taste to the air that hints of winter. I am busy in this season when people fling open the doors of their life's closet and decide that they must make a change, stand up for themselves, perhaps tackle a problem they have let fester, hidden, for far too long. I feel the joy of fixing things, of making them right.

I sit in the cockpit and look out on the creek. I have learned many things about myself in this last year. I know now that my capacity for love did not die with Ryan. I know that I am a better person than I gave myself credit for and still not as good a person as I should become. I understand that the future is unpredictable, that you cannot plan for it, but you must meet it bravely nevertheless.

Letting Michael go was difficult. In the end, I told him the truth as far as I could—that a relationship must be based on trust, and I had kept things from him that I would never share. It was an awkward, painful conversation, one I will not replay. If he had told me it didn't matter, that he could accept I had secrets and still love me, perhaps I could have been convinced. But that is not who he is, and given the past, I cannot blame him. Sometimes I am sorry he let me go so easily. Sometimes I dream I am on the dock and hear him call my name, and I turn to see him standing there, smiling, and little Lizzie is running toward me, hair flying, while I open my arms. But it is just a dream.

And life goes on.

About the Author

Ann Eichenmuller has always had a love affair with words. Born in Baltimore, Maryland in 1960, she created stories before she could read or write. Her family was her captive audience, a role they did not always relish.

"My grandmother once offered me 25 cents if I would keep quiet for five minutes," she laughs.

She spent her childhood scribbling fiction, and in high school created "Search for Sanity, "a serial soap opera written to entertain her friends. Ann went on to attend St. Mary's College of Maryland, where she was inspired by Dr. Michael Glaser (Maryland's Poet Laureate) to take on the editorship of the school's literary magazine. It was at St. Mary's that she also met and married fellow student Eric Eichenmuller, a musician and songwriter with whom she later co-wrote the musical All Good Gifts based on O. Henry's "The Gift of the Magi." After graduating with a B.A. in English in 1982, Ann accepted a teaching position with St. Mary's County Schools.

"I wanted share the taste of words, the smell of them, the way they feel as they roll off of your tongue," she says, adding she also wanted her students to realize "that words have incredible power."

Her efforts earned her two Teacher of the Year Awards as well as the prestigious Washington Post's Agnes Meyer Award for Excellence in 1999. Despite long hours developing lesson plans and editing papers, Ann still found a creative outlet in writing plays for her students to perform. In these she explored the serious issues facing adolescents in modern society.

When they weren't working, Ann and Eric spent their time camping and sailing with their three children. In 1996 the couple purchased a cruising sailboat, and less than a year later, they set sail from Cobb Island, Maryland for the Bahamas. Ann celebrated their adventure in her first-ever non-fiction piece, "A Life Less Ordinary" published in *Spin Sheet* magazine in 1997.

In the next few years Ann found the time to publish two short stories. She and Eric also became certified divers, licensed private pilots, and proud owners of their Piper Cherokee airplane. Then in 2007, with their children grown, they came up with a new life plan.

"Our saying became, 'How long do you live?' It's an answer you can't know. It propelled us to do what we really wanted," Ann says.

That meant selling their house, moving aboard their boat, and buying an 1886 farmhouse on Virginia's Northern Neck. Their goal? An early retirement and a second chance to pursue their dreams. They spent seven years of weekends renovating the house, and meanwhile Ann also completed her M.A. in Humanities. In 2014 the plan was completed, and Ann returned to her writing.

With Eric's encouragement, she responded to an ad in All at Sea for "inkslingers" and pitched her first essay. She still remembers the thrill of that acceptance–and that first check.

"I was just so excited that someone was willing to pay me for what I wrote!" she laughs.

Encouraged by her success, she pitched article ideas to other magazines, eventually landing regular spots in *Chesapeake Bay and Motorhome*. She also joined a local writers' group, whose members she credits with getting her beyond the "20,000 word barrier." In 2017 her first novel, *Kind Lies*, was published by High Tide Publications. Now she hopes to finish one of the other three unfinished manuscripts she's working on, but her main focus is to continue growing both as a writer and a person.

"Then I know I'll have no regrets."

Made in the USA
Lexington, KY
28 March 2017